Praise for *The Sisterhood of the Traveling Pants*

☆ "An outstanding and vivid book that will stay with readers for a long time. Readers will hope that Brashares chronicles the sisterhood for volumes to come." —*Publishers Weekly*, Starred, Flying Start

☆ "A complex book about a solid group of friends, with each one a strong and courageous individual in her own right. They form a true sisterhood of acceptance and support, resulting in a believable and inviting world."
—*School Library Journal*, Starred

"The loving depiction of enduring and solid friendship will ring true to readers, who will appreciate this recognition of one of life's most important relationships."
—*The Bulletin of the Center for Children's Books*, Recommended

"The collective heroines . . . are winning and precocious. Their story zips along, bouncing faster than the jeans from girl to girl . . . wonderfully detailed."
—*The New York Times Book Review*

"Funny, memorable, and touching, this book is one that the reader will not want to end." —*Voice of Youth Advocates*

"A posse of loyal girlfriends has enormous appeal; add in the dream-come-true perfect pair of jeans and you can't lose. Good friends, like good pants, should make you feel fabulous; Brashares takes the two and creates a breezy, feel-good book." —*The Horn Book Magazine*

Also by Ann Brashares
The Second Summer of the Sisterhood
Girls in Pants: The Third Summer of the Sisterhood

The Sisterhood

of the

Traveling Pants

Ann Brashares

Published by Dell Laurel-Leaf
an imprint of Random House Children's Books
a division of Random House, Inc.
New York

This is a work of fiction. Names, characters, places, and incidents either
are the product of the author's imagination or are used fictitiously. Any
resemblance to actual persons, living or dead, events, or locales is entirely
coincidental.

Originally published in hardcover in the United States of America by
Delacorte Press, New York, in 2001. This edition published by arrangement
with Delacorte Press.

Dell and Laurel are registered trademarks of Random House, Inc.

Produced by Alloy Entertainment
151 West 26th Street
New York, NY 10001

www.randomhouse.com/teens

Educators and librarians, for a variety of teaching tools, visit us at
www.randomhouse.com/teachers

ISBN: 978-0-375-85420-0
May 2006
Printed in the United States of America
10 9 8 7 6 5 4 3 2 1

For Jodi Anderson,
the real thing

Acknowledgments

I would like to thank Wendy Loggia, Beverly Horowitz, Leslie Morgenstein, Josh Bank, Russell Gordon, Lauren Monchik, Marci Senders, and of course, Jodi Anderson, the true muse.

I would also like to thank Jacob Collins, Jane Easton Brashares, and William Brashares and to lovingly acknowledge Sam, Nathaniel, and the little one soon to be born.

We, the sisterhood, hereby instate the following rules to govern the use of the Traveling Pants:

1. You must never wash the Pants.

2. You must never double-cuff the Pants. It's tacky. There will never be a time when this will not be tacky.

3. You must never say the word "phat" while wearing the Pants. You must also never think "I am fat" while wearing the Pants.

4. You must never let a boy take off the Pants (although you may take them off yourself in his presence).

5. You must not pick your nose while wearing the Pants. You may, however, scratch casually at your nostril while really kind of picking.

6. Upon our reunion, you must follow the proper procedures for documenting your time in the Pants.

7. You must write to your Sisters throughout the summer, no matter how much fun you are having without them.

8. You must pass the Pants along to your Sisters according to the specifications set down by the Sisterhood. Failure to comply will result in a severe spanking upon our reunion.

9. You must not wear the Pants with a tucked-in shirt and belt. See rule #2.

10. Remember: Pants = love. Love your pals. Love yourself.

Not all who wander are lost.

–J.R.R. Tolkien

PROLOGUE

Once upon a time there was a pair of pants. They were an essential kind of pants—jeans, naturally, blue but not that stiff, new blue that you see so often on the first day of school. They were a soft, changeable blue with a little extra fading at the knees and the seat and white wavelets at the cuffs.

They'd had a good life before us. You could just tell. I guess a thrift shop is like the pound in some ways. Whatever you get there owes a lot to its previous owners. Our pants weren't like the neurotic puppy whose parents left it alone, barking itself hoarse from morning till night. They were more like the grown-up dog whose family loved it but had to move to an apartment building or maybe to Korea (is it Korea?), where people sometimes eat dogs.

I could tell the pants hadn't come to our lives because of tragedy. They'd just witnessed one of those regular but painful life transitions. That, it turns out, is The Way of the Pants.

They were noble pants, but unassuming. You could glance over them and just think, "Okay, pants," or you could stop and really look at the beautiful complexity of colors and seams. They don't force you to admire them. They are happy just doing their basic job of covering your butt without making it look fatter than it actually is.

I got them at a thrift shop at the outer reaches of Georgetown that's sandwiched between a store that sells water (I don't know about you, but I get that free at home) and a health food store called Yes! Whenever any of us mentions Yes! (and we work it in whenever possible) we always shout Yes! at the top of our lungs. I was tagging along with Lena and her younger sister, Effie, and their mom. Effie was there to buy a dress for the sophomore prom. Effie isn't the kind of girl who just gets a red spaghetti-strap thing at Bloomingdale's like everybody else. She has to get something *vintage*.

Mainly I got the pants because Lena's mom hates secondhand clothing stores. She says used clothes are for poor people. "I tink that is dirty, Effie," she kept saying every time Effie pulled something off a hanger. I secretly agreed with Mrs. Kaligaris, which gave me a certain feeling of shame. Truth was, I yearned for the clean mind-lessness of Express, but I had to buy something. The pants were folded innocently on a shelf by the counter where you pay. I figured maybe they'd been washed. Also, they were only $3.49 including tax. I didn't even try them on, so you can tell I wasn't serious about owning them. My butt has specific requirements for pants.

Effie picked out a little mod dress that was aggressively antiprom, and Lena found a pair of beat-up loafers that looked like they'd belonged to somebody's great-uncle. Lena has big feet, like size nine and a half or something. They are the only part of her that isn't perfect. I love her feet. I couldn't help wincing at those shoes, though. It's bad enough to buy used clothes, which are theoretically wash-able, but *used shoes?*

When I got home I put the pants in the back of my closet and forgot about them.

They came out again the afternoon before we all went separate ways for the summer. I was going to South Carolina to hang out with my dad, Lena and Effie were spending two months in Greece with their grandparents, Bridget was fly-ing off to soccer camp in Baja California (which, turns out, is in Mexico. Who knew?). Tibby was staying home. This was our first summer apart, and I think it gave us all a strange, shaky feeling.

Last summer we'd all taken American history, because Lena said you could get a better grade in the summer. I'm sure Lena did get a better grade. The summer before that we were all CITs at Camp Tall Timbers on the eastern shore of Maryland. Bridget coached soccer and taught swimming, Lena worked in arts and crafts, and Tibby was stuck in the kitchen once again. I helped in the drama workshop until I lost my temper at two demonic nine-year-olds and got reassigned to the camp office to lick envelopes by myself. They would have fired me straight out, but I think our parents actually paid them to have us work there.

The summers before that are a blur of baby oil and Sun-In and hating our bodies (I got big breasts; Tibby got no breasts) at the Rockwood public swimming pool. My skin got darker, but not one strand of my hair turned the promised blond.

And I guess before that . . . God, I don't know what we did. Tibby went to a socialist day camp for a while and helped build low-income houses. Bridget had a lot of tennis lessons. Lena and Effie splashed around in their pool day after day. I think I watched a lot of TV, to be honest. Still, we managed to find one another for at least a few hours a day, and on the weekends we were never apart. There are the years that stand out: the summer

Lena's family built the pool, the summer Bridget got chicken pox and gave it to the rest of us. The summer my dad moved away.

For some reason our lives were marked by summers. While Lena and I went to public elementary school, Bridget went to a private school with a bunch of other jocks, and Tibby was still going to Embrace, this tiny, weird school where the kids sat in beanbag chairs instead of desks and nobody got any grades. Summer was the time when our lives joined completely, when we all had our birthdays, when really important things happened. Except for the year Bridget's mom died. That happened at Christmastime.

We started being "we" before we were born. We were all four born at the end of summer, within seventeen days of one another: Lena first, at the end of August, and me last, in the middle of September. It's not so much a coincidence, as the reason we started.

The summer we were born our mothers took a class in aerobics for pregnant women (just picture that) at this place called Gilda's; they were the September group (Lena came a little early). Aerobics was really popular then. I guess the other members of the class weren't due to pop till the winter, but the Septembers were so dramatically pregnant, the teacher was worried they might explode at any moment. The teacher would alter the routines for them. "Septembers!" she would bellow, according to my mother. "Just do four reps; watch it! Watch it!" The aerobics instructor's name happened to be April, and as my mother tells it, they hated that woman.

The Septembers started hanging out after class, complaining about their swollen feet and how fat they were and laughing about April. After we were born—miraculously all girls, plus Bridget's twin brother—they formed their own little mothers' support group and let us all squirm on a blanket together while they complained about not sleeping and how fat they still were. The support group disbanded after a while, but the summers when we were one and two and three they'd still bring us to Rockwood. We'd pee in the baby pool and take one another's toys.

The friendships between our mothers sort of deteriorated after that. I'm not sure why. Their lives got complicated, I guess. A couple of them went back to work. Tibby's parents moved to that farm way out on Rockville Pike. Maybe our mothers never really had much in common besides being pregnant at the same time. I mean, they were a strange group when you think of it: Tibby's mom, the young radical; Lena's mom, the ambitious Greek putting herself through social work school; Bridget's mom, the Alabama debutante; and my mom, the Puerto Rican with the rocky marriage. But for a while there, they seemed like friends. I can even remember it a little.

Nowadays our mothers act like friendship is an elective—falling somewhere down the list after husbands, children, career, home, money. Somewhere between outdoor grilling and music appreciation. That's not how it is for us. My mom tells me, "Just wait till you get serious about boys and school. Just wait till you start competing." But she's wrong. We won't let that happen to us.

Eventually our mothers' friendship stopped being about them and came to be about us, the daughters. They became sort of like divorced people, with not much in common but the kids and the past. To tell the truth, they are awkward with one another—especially after what happened to Bridget's mom. It's like there are disappointments and maybe even a few secrets between them, so they just stay on the fragile surface.

We're the Septembers now. The real ones. We are everything to one another. We don't need to say so; it's just true. Sometimes it seems like we're so close we form one single complete person rather than four separate ones. We settle into types—Bridget the athlete, Lena the beauty, Tibby the rebel, and me, Carmen, the . . . what?

The one with the bad temper. But the one who cares the most. The one who cares that we stick together.

You know what the secret is? It's so simple. We love one another. We're nice to one another. Do you know how rare that is?

My mother says it can't stay like this, but I believe it will. The Pants are like an omen. They stand for the promise we made to one another, that no matter what happens, we stick together. But they stand for a challenge too. It's not enough to stay in Bethesda, Maryland, and hunker down in air-conditioned houses. We promised one another that someday we'd get out in the world and figure some stuff out.

I can pretend to be a deep, faithful, and instant appreciator of the Pants, or I can be honest and tell you that I was the one who almost threw them away. But that requires backing up a little and telling you how the Traveling Pants were born.

Luck never gives;
it only lends.
—Ancient chinese
proverb

"Can you close that suitcase?" Tibby asked Carmen. "It's making me sick."

Carmen glanced at the structured canvas bag splayed wantonly in the middle of her bed. Suddenly she wished she had all-new underwear. Her best satin pair was sprouting tiny ropes of elastic from the waistband.

"It's making *me* sick," Lena said. "I haven't started packing. My flight's at seven."

Carmen flopped the top of the suitcase closed and sat down on the carpeted floor. She was working on removing navy-blue polish from her toenails.

"Lena, could you not say that word anymore?" Tibby asked, wilting a little on the edge of Carmen's bed. "It's making me sick."

"Which word?" Bridget asked. "Packing? Flight? Seven?"

Tibby considered. "All of them."

"Oh, Tibs," Carmen said, grabbing Tibby's foot from where she sat. "It's gonna be okay."

Tibby took her foot back. "It's gonna be okay for you. You're going away. You're going to eat barbecue all the time and light firecrackers and everything."

Tibby had nonsensical ideas about what people did in South Carolina, but Carmen knew not to argue with her.

Lena let out a little hum of sympathy.

Tibby turned on her. "Don't make that pity noise, Lena."

Lena cleared her throat. "I didn't," she said quickly, even though she had.

"Don't wallow," Bridget urged Tibby. "You're wallowing."

"No," Tibby shot back. She held up hands crossed at the wrist in a hex sign to ward off Bridget. "No pep talks. No fair. I only let you do pep talks when *you* need to feel better."

"I wasn't doing a pep talk," Bridget said defensively, even though she was.

Carmen made her wise eyebrows. "Hey, Tibs? Maybe if you're nasty enough, you won't miss us and we won't miss you."

"Carma!" Tibby shouted, getting to her feet and thrusting a stiff arm at Carmen. "I see through that! You're doing psychological analysis on me. No! No!"

Carmen's cheeks flushed. "I am not," she said quietly.

The three of them sat, scolded into silence.

"God, Tibby, what is anybody allowed to say?" Bridget asked.

Tibby thought about it. "You can say . . ." She glanced around the room. She had tears welling in her eyes, but Carmen knew she didn't want them to show. "You can say . . ." Her eyes lighted on the pair of pants folded on the top of a stack of clothes on Carmen's dresser. "You can say, 'Hey, Tibby, want those pants?'"

Carmen looked baffled. She capped the polish remover, walked over to her dresser, and held up the pants. Tibby usually liked clothes that were ugly or challenging. These were just jeans. "You mean these?" They were creased in three places from inattention.

Tibby nodded sullenly. "Those."

"You really want them?" Carmen didn't feel like mentioning that she was planning to throw them away. Bigger points if they mattered.

"Uh-huh."

Tibby was demanding a little display of unconditional love. Then again, it was her right. Three of them were flying off on big adventures the next day, and Tibby was launching her career at Wallman's in scenic Bethesda for five cents over minimum wage.

"Fine," Carmen said benevolently, handing them over.

Tibby absently hugged the pants, slightly deflated at getting her way so fast.

Lena studied them. "Are those the pants you got at the secondhand place next to Yes!?"

"Yes!" Carmen shouted back.

Tibby unfolded them. "They're great."

The pants suddenly looked different to Carmen. Now that somebody cared about them, they looked a little nicer.

"Don't you think you should try them on?" Lena asked practically. "If they fit Carmen, they aren't going to fit you."

Carmen and Tibby both glared at Lena, not sure who should take more offense.

"What?" Bridget said, hopping to Lena's aid. "You guys have completely different builds. Is that not obvious?"

"Fine," Tibby said, glad to be huffy again.

Tibby pulled off her dilapidated brown cargo pants, revealing lavender cotton underwear. She turned her back to her friends for the sake of drama as she pulled on the pants. She zipped, buttoned, and turned around. "Ta-da!"

Lena studied her. "Wow."

"Tibs, you're such a babe," Bridget proclaimed.

Tibby tried not to let her smile get loose. She

went over to the mirror and turned to the side. "You think they're good?"

"Are those really my pants?" Carmen asked.

Tibby had narrow hips and long legs for her small frame. The pants fell below her waist, hugging her hips intimately. They revealed a white strip of flat stomach, a nice inny belly button.

"You look like a girl," Bridget added.

Tibby didn't quarrel. She knew as well as anyone that she looked skinny and shapeless in the oversized pants she usually wore.

The pants bagged a little at her feet, but that worked for Tibby.

Suddenly Tibby looked unsure. "I don't know. Maybe somebody else should try them." Slowly she unbuttoned and unzipped.

"Tibby, you are crazy," Carmen said. "Those pants are in love with you. They want you for your body and your mind." She couldn't help seeing the pants in a completely new way.

Tibby threw them at Lena. "Here. You go."

"Why? They're meant to be yours," Lena argued.

Tibby shrugged. "Just try them."

Carmen could see Lena glancing at the pants with a certain amount of interest. "Why not? Lena, try 'em."

Lena looked at the pants warily. She shed her own khakis and pulled them on. She made sure they were buttoned and sitting straight on her hips before she glanced in the mirror.

Bridget considered.

"Lenny, you make me sick," Tibby offered.

"Jesus, Lena," Carmen said. *Sorry, Jesus*, she added to herself reflexively.

"They're *nice pants*," Lena said reverently, almost whispering.

They were used to Lena, but Carmen knew that to the rest of the world she was fairly stunning. She had Mediterranean skin that tanned well, straight, shiny dark hair, and wide eyes roughly the color of celery. Her face was so lovely, so delicately structured, it kind of gave Carmen a stomachache. Carmen once confessed her worry to Tibby that some movie director was going to spot Lena and take her away, and Tibby admitted she had worried the exact same thing. Particularly beautiful people were like particularly funny-looking people, though. Once you knew them you mostly forgot about it.

The pants clung to Lena's waist and followed the line of her hips. They held close to the shape of her thighs and fell exactly to the tops of her feet. When she took two steps forward, they appeared to hug each of her muscles as they shifted and moved. Carmen gazed in wonder at how different was their effect from Lena's bland uniform of J. Crew khakis.

"Very sexy," Bridget said.

Lena snatched another peek at the mirror. She always held herself in a slightly awkward way, with her neck pushed forward, when she looked in a mirror. She winced. "I think maybe they're too tight," she said.

"Are you joking?" Tibby barked. "They are beautiful. They look a million times better than those lame-o pants you usually wear."

Lena turned to Tibby. "Was that a compliment somewhere in there?"

"Seriously, you have to have them," Tibby said. "They're like . . . transforming."

Lena fiddled with the waistband. She was never comfortable talking about the way she looked.

"You are always beautiful," Carmen added. "But Tibby's right . . . you look . . . just . . . different."

Lena slid the pants off her hips. "Bee has to try them."

"I do?"

"You do," Lena confirmed.

"She's too tall for them," Tibby said.

"Just try," Lena said.

"I don't need any more jeans," Bridget said. "I have, like, nine pairs."

"What, are you scared of them?" Carmen taunted. Stupid dares like that always worked on Bridget.

17

Bridget grabbed them from Lena. She took off her dark indigo jeans, kicked them into a pile on the floor, and pulled on the pants. At first she tried to pull the pants way up on her waist, so they would be too short, but as soon as she let go, the pants settled gracefully on her hips.

"Doo-doo-doo-doo," Carmen sang, hitting the notes of the *Twilight Zone* theme.

Bridget turned around to look at her backside. "What?"

"They're not short; they're perfect," Lena said.

Tibby cocked her head, studying Bridget carefully. "You look almost . . . small, Bee. Not your usual Amazon."

"The insult parade marches on," Lena said, laughing.

Bridget was tall, with broad shoulders and long legs and big hands. It was easy to think she was a big person, but she was surprisingly narrow through her hips and waist.

"She's right," Carmen said. "The pants fit better than your usual ones."

Bridget switched her butt in front of the mirror. "These do look good," she said. "Wow. I think I may love them."

"You've got a great little butt," Carmen pointed out.

Tibby laughed. "That from the queen of butts."

She got a troublemaking look in her eyes. "Hey. You know how we find out if these pants are truly magical?"

"How?" Carmen asked.

Tibby jiggled her foot in the air. "You try them on. I know they're yours and all, but I'm just saying, scientifically speaking, that it is impossible for these pants to fit you too."

Carmen chewed the inside of her cheek. "Are you casting aspersions on my butt?"

"Oh, Carma. You know I envy it. I just don't think these pants are going to fit over it," Tibby explained reasonably.

Bridget and Lena nodded.

Suddenly Carmen was afraid that the pants that hugged each of her friends' bodies with loving grace would not fit over her upper thighs. She wasn't really chubby, but she had inherited her backside directly from the Puerto Rican half of the family. It was very nicely shaped, and most days she felt proud of it, but here with these pants and her three little-assed friends, she didn't feel like standing out like the big fatso.

"Nah. I don't want them," Carmen said, standing up and getting ready to try to change the subject. Six eyes remained fixed on the pants.

"Yes," Bridget said. "You have to."

"Please, Carmen?" Lena asked.

She saw too much anticipation on her friends'

faces to drop it without a fight. "Fine. Don't expect them to fit or anything. I'm sure they won't."

"Carmen, they're *your* pants," Bridget pointed out.

"Yeah, smarty, but I never tried them on before." Carmen said it with enough force to ward off further questions. She pulled off her black flares and pulled on the jeans. They didn't stop at her thighs. They went right up over her hips without complaint. She fastened them. "So?" She wasn't ready to venture a look in the mirror yet.

Nobody said anything.

"What?" Carmen felt cursed. "What? Are they that bad?" She found the courage to meet Tibby's eye. "What?"

"I . . . I just . . ." Tibby trailed off.

"Oh my," Lena said quietly.

Carmen winced and looked away. "I'll just take them off, and we'll pretend this never happened," she said, her cheeks flushing.

Bridget found words. "Carmen, that's not it at all! Look at yourself! You are a thing of beauty. You are a vision. You are a supermodel."

Carmen put her hand on her hip and made a sour face. "That I doubt."

"Seriously. Look at yourself," Lena ordered. "These are magic pants."

Carmen looked at herself. First from far away,

then from up close. From the front and then the back.

The CD they'd been listening to ended, but nobody seemed to notice. The phone was ringing distantly, but nobody got up to get it. The normally busy street was silent.

Carmen finally let out her breath. "These are magic pants."

*　　*　　*

It was Bridget's idea. The discovery of magical pants on such a day, right before their first summer apart, warranted a trip to Gilda's. Tibby got the food and picked up her movie camera, Carmen brought the bad eighties dance music, Lena supplied the atmospherics. Bridget brought the large-sized bobby pins and the Pants. They handled the parents issue in their usual way—Carmen told her mom she'd be at Lena's, Lena told her mom she'd be at Tibby's, Tibby told her mom she'd be at Bridget's, and Bridget asked her brother to tell her dad she'd be at Carmen's. Bridget spent so much time at her friends' houses, it was doubtful that Perry would pass on the message or that her father would think to be concerned, but it was part of the tradition.

They all met up again at the entrance on Wisconsin Avenue at nine forty-five. The place was dark and closed of course, which was where the bobby pins came in. They all watched breathlessly as Bridget expertly jimmied the lock. They'd done this at least once a year for the last three years, but the breaking-in part never got less exciting. Luckily, Gilda's security remained as lame as ever. What was there to steal anyway? Smelly blue mats? A box of rusty, mismatched free weights?

The lock clicked, the doorknob turned, and they all raced up the stairs to the second floor, purposefully revving up a little hysteria in the black stairwell. Lena set up the blankets and the candles. Tibby laid out the food—raw cookie dough from a refrigerated tube, strawberry Pop-Tarts with pink icing, the hard, deformed kind of cheese puffs, sour Gummi Worms, and a few bottles of Odwalla. Carmen set up the music, starting with an awful and ancient Paula Abdul tune, while Bridget leaped around in front of the mirrored wall.

"I think this was your mom's spot, Lenny," Bridget called, bouncing again and again on an indented floorboard.

"Funny," Lena said. There was a famous picture of the four moms in their eighties aerobics gear with their stomachs sticking out, and Lena's mom was by far the hugest. Lena weighed more at birth than Bridget and her brother, Perry, put together.

"Ready?" Carmen turned the music down and placed the Pants ceremonially in the middle of the blanket.

Lena was still lighting candles.

"Bee, come on," Carmen shouted at Bridget, who was laughing at herself in front of the mirror.

When they were all gathered and Bridget stopped aerobicizing, Carmen began. "On the last night before the diaspora"—she paused briefly so everyone could admire her use of the word—"we discovered some magic." She felt an itchy tingle in the arches of her feet. "Magic comes in many forms. Tonight it comes to us in a pair of pants. I hereby propose that these Pants belong to us equally, that they will travel to all the places we're going, and they will keep us together when we are apart."

"Let's take the vow of the Traveling Pants." Bridget excitedly grabbed Lena's and Tibby's hands. Bridget and Carmen were always the ones who staged friendship ceremonies unabashedly. Tibby and Lena were the ones who acted like there was a camera crew in the room.

"Tonight we are Sisters of the Pants," Bridget intoned when they'd formed a ring. "Tonight we give the Pants the love of our Sisterhood so we can take that love wherever we go."

The candles flickered in the big, high-ceilinged room.

Lena looked solemn. Tibby's face showed that she was struggling, but Carmen couldn't tell whether it was against laughter or tears.

"We should write down the rules," Lena suggested. "So we know what to do with them—you know, like who gets them when."

They all agreed, so Bridget stole a piece of Gilda's stationery and a pen from the little office.

They ate snacks, and Tibby filmed for posterity, while they constructed the rules. The Manifesto, as Carmen called it. "I feel like a founding father," she said importantly. Lena was nominated to write it, because she had the best handwriting.

The rules took a while to sort out. Lena and Carmen wanted to focus on friendship-type rules, stuff about keeping in touch with one another over the summer, and making sure the Pants kept moving from one girl to the next. Tibby preferred to focus on random things you could and couldn't do in the Pants—like picking your nose. Bridget had the idea of inscribing the Pants with memories of the summer once they were all together again. By the time they'd agreed on ten rules, Lena held a motley list that ranged from sincere to silly. Carmen knew they would stick to them.

Next, they talked about how long each of them should have the Pants before passing them on, finally deciding that each person should send them on when she felt the time was right. But to keep the Pants moving, no one should keep them for over a week unless she really needed to. This meant that the Pants could possibly make the rounds twice before the end of the summer.

"Lena should have them first," Bridget said, tying two Gummi Worms together and biting off the sticky knot. "Greece is a good place to start."

"Can it be me next?" Tibby asked. "I'll be the one needing them to pull me out of my depression." Lena nodded sympathetically.

After that would be Carmen. Then Bridget. Then, just to mix things up, the Pants would bounce back in the opposite direction. From Bridget to Carmen to Tibby and back to Lena.

As they talked, midnight came to divide their last day together from their first day apart. There was a thrill in the air, and Carmen could see from her friends' faces that she wasn't the only one who felt it. The Pants seemed to be infused with the promises of the summer. This would be Carmen's first whole summer with her dad since she was a kid. She could picture herself with him, laughing it up, making him laugh, wearing the Pants.

In solemnity Lena laid the manifesto on top of the Pants. Bridget called for a moment of silence. "To honor the Pants," she said.

"And the Sisterhood," Lena added.

Carmen felt tiny bumps rising along her arms. "And this moment. And this summer. And the rest of our lives."

"Together and apart," Tibby finished.

We, the Sisterhood, hereby instate the following rules to govern the use of the Traveling Pants:

1. You must never wash the Pants.

2. You must never double-cuff the Pants. It's tacky. There will never be a time when this will not be tacky.

3. You must never say the word "phat" while wearing the Pants. You must also never think "I am fat" while wearing the Pants.

4. You must never let a boy take off the Pants (although you may take them off yourself in his presence).

5. You must not pick your nose while wearing the Pants. You may, however, scratch casually at your nostril while really kind of picking.

6. Upon our reunion, you must follow the proper procedures for documenting your time in the Pants:
   - On the left leg of the Pants, write the most exciting place you have been while wearing the Pants.

- On the right leg of the Pants, write the most important thing that has happened to you while wearing the Pants. (For example, "I hooked up with my second cousin, Ivan, while wearing the Traveling Pants.")

7. You must write to your Sisters throughout the summer, no matter how much fun you are having without them.

8. You must pass the Pants along to your Sisters according to the specifications set down by the Sisterhood. Failure to comply will result in a severe spanking upon our reunion.

9. You must not wear the Pants with a tucked-in shirt and belt. See rule #2.

10. Remember: Pants = love. Love your pals. Love yourself.

Today is the
tomorrow we worried
about yesterday.
—Anonymous

One day, around the time Tibby was twelve, she realized she could judge her happiness by her guinea pig, Mimi. When she was feeling busy, full of plans and purpose, she raced out of her room, past Mimi's glass box, feeling faintly sad that Mimi just had to lie there lumpen in her wood shavings while Tibby's life was so big.

She could tell she was miserable when she stared at Mimi with envy, wishing it was her who got to drink fat water droplets from a dispenser positioned at exactly the height of her mouth. Wishing it was her who could snuggle into the warm shavings and decide only whether to spin a few rotations on her exercise wheel or just take another nap. No decisions, no disappointments.

Tibby got Mimi when she was seven. At the time she thought Mimi was the most beautiful name in the world. She had saved it up for almost a year, waiting. It was very easy to spend your best name on a stuffed animal or on an imaginary friend. But Tibby held out. Those were the days when Tibby trusted what she liked. Later, if she loved the name Mimi, she would have thought that was a good reason to name her Frederick.

Today, with her green Wallman's smock crushed under her arm, with no one to complain to, with no good things to look forward to, Tibby was purely jealous.

Nobody ever sent a guinea pig off to work, did they? She imagined Mimi in a matching smock. Mimi was hopelessly unproductive.

A howl rose from the kitchen, reminding Tibby of two other unproductive creatures in the house — her two-year-old brother and one-year-old sister. They were all noise and destruction and evil-smelling diapers. Even Wallman's drugstore seemed like a sanctuary compared to her house at lunchtime.

She packed her digital movie camera in its bag and put it on a high shelf in case Nicky found his way into her room again. She stuck one piece of masking tape over the Power button of her computer and another longer piece over the CD drive. Nicky loved turning her computer off and jamming discs into the slot.

"I'm going to work," she called to Loretta, the baby-sitter, heading down the stairs and straight out the front door. She never liked to phrase her plans as questions, because she didn't want Loretta to think she had jurisdiction over Tibby.

Many going-to-be juniors had their licenses. Tibby had her bike. She rode the first block trying to pin her smock and wallet under her arm, but she had trouble maneuvering. She stopped. The one reasonable solution was to wear the smock and put the wallet in the pocket of her smock. She stuffed them back under her arm and kept riding.

At Brissard Lane her wallet came unpinned from her arm and bounced on the street. She nearly rode into a moving car. She stopped again and retrieved her wallet.

With a quick look around, she determined she'd see no one she knew in the four blocks between here and Wallman's. She pulled the smock over her head, stuck the wallet in the pocket, and rode like the wind.

"Yo, Tibby," she heard a familiar voice call as she turned into the parking lot. Her heart sank. She longed for the wood shavings. "Whassup?"

It was Tucker Rowe, who was, in her opinion, the hottest junior at Westmoreland. For the summer he'd grown an excellent soul patch just under his lower lip. He was standing by his car, an antique seventies muscle car that practically made her swoon.

Tibby couldn't look at him. The smock was burning her body. She kept her head down while she locked her bike. She ducked into the store, hoping maybe he'd think he'd been mistaken, that maybe the loser girl in the polyester smock with the little darts for breasts was not the actual Tibby, but a much less cool facsimile.

Dear Bee,
    I'm enclosing a very small square cut from the lining of my smock. In part, I enjoyed maiming the garment, and in part, I just wanted you to see how thick 2-ply polyester really is.
Tibby

"Vreeland, Bridget?" the camp director, Connie Broward, read off her clipboard.

Bridget was already standing. She couldn't sit anymore. She couldn't keep her feet still. "Right here!" she called. She hitched her duffel bag over one shoulder and her backpack over the other. A warm breeze blew off Bahía Concepción. You could actually see the turquoise bay from the central camp building. She felt the excitement rising in her veins.

"Cabin four, follow Sherrie," Connie instructed.

Bridget could feel lots of eyes on her, but she didn't dwell on it. She was used to people looking at her. She knew that her hair was unusual. It was long and straight and the color of a peeled banana. People always made a big deal about her hair. Also she was tall and her features were regular — her nose straight, all the things in the right places. The combination of qualities made people mistake her for beautiful.

She wasn't beautiful. Not like Lena. There was no particular poetry or grace in her face. She knew that, and she knew that other people probably realized that too, once they got over her hair.

"Hi, I'm Bridget," she said to Sherrie, throwing her stuff down on the bed Sherrie pointed to.

"Welcome," Sherrie said. "How far did you come?"

"From Washington, D.C.," Bridget answered.

"That's a long way."

It was. Bridget had awoken at four A.M. to catch a six o'clock flight to Los Angeles, then a two-hour flight from LAX to the minuscule airport in Loreto, a town on the Sea of Cortez on the eastern coast of the Baja peninsula. Then there had been a van ride — just long enough for her to fall deeply asleep and wake up disoriented.

Sherrie moved on to the next arriving camper. The cabin contained fourteen simple metal-frame twin beds, each with one thin mattress. The interior was unfinished, made of badly joined planks of pine.

Bridget moved outside to the tiny porch at the front of the cabin.

If the inside was standard-issue camp, the outside was magical. The camp faced a wide cove of white sand and palm trees. The bay was so perfectly blue, it looked like it had been retouched for a tourist brochure. Across the bay stood protective mountains, shoulder to shoulder, across the Concepción peninsula.

At the back of the camp buildings stood shorter, craggier hills. Miraculously, somebody had managed to carve out two beautiful full-sized soccer fields, irrigated to an even, glowing green, between the beach and the arid hills.

"Hi. Hi." Bridget waved to two girls lugging their stuff into the cabin. They had tan, muscular soccer-player legs.

Bridget followed them into the cabin. Almost all the beds were claimed. "You want to go swimming?" she asked. Bridget wasn't afraid of strangers. Often she liked them better than people she knew.

"I've got to unpack," one of the girls said.

"I think we're supposed to go to dinner in a couple of minutes," the other one said.

"Okay," Bridget said easily. "I'm Bridget, by the way. See you later," she called over her shoulder.

She changed into her bathing suit in an outside shower and ventured out onto the sand. The air felt

34

the exact temperature of her skin. The water held all the colors of the sunset. Fading sun rays touched her shoulders as they disappeared behind the hills. She dove in and stayed under a long time.

I'm happy to be here, Bridget thought. Her mind flicked for a split second to Lena and the Traveling Pants—to how she couldn't wait to get ahold of them and live her own story in them.

A little while later, when she arrived at dinner, she was thrilled to see long tables set up on the big, simple deck off the side of the cafeteria building, instead of crammed in under the low ceiling inside. A wig of dense magenta bougainvillea drooped from the roof and crept along the railings. It seemed crazy to spend even a minute indoors here.

Tonight she sat with the rest of cabin four. There were a total of six cabins, which she quickly calculated to mean eighty-four girls, all of whom were serious athletes. You couldn't come here if you weren't. She would know, and possibly even care about, these girls by the end, but tonight they were hard to keep track of. She was pretty sure the one with the dark, shoulder-length hair was Emily. The girl with the frizzy blond hair across from her was Olivia, called Ollie. Next to Ollie was an African American girl with hair down to the middle of her back, named Diana.

Over seafood tacos, huge mounds of rice and

beans, and lemonade that tasted as though it was made from powder, Connie stood at a makeshift podium and talked about her years on the U.S. Women's Olympic Team. Spread among the tables were various coaches and trainers.

Back in her cabin, Bridget crawled into her sleeping bag and stared at the crack of moonlight reaching through two planks of wood in the ceiling. Suddenly it occurred to her: She was in Baja. Why should she grasp for a crack of the sky when she could have the whole thing? She got up and bunched her sleeping bag and pillow under her arm.

"Anybody want to sleep on the beach?" she asked the group.

There was a pause and scattered discussion.

"Are we allowed to?" Emily asked.

"I never heard that we weren't," Bridget answered. It wasn't crucial to her plans that anyone follow her, but it was also fine when two others did—Diana and another girl named Jo.

They set up their sleeping bags at the edge of the wide beach. Who knew how high the tide came? The gentle sound of the surf beat away on the beach. The stars spread out above them, glorious.

Bridget was so joyful, so full, it was hard to make herself lie down in the sleeping bag. She heard herself sigh at the pulsing sky spread out above her. "I love this."

Jo dug deeper into her sleeping bag. "It is unbelievable."

For a while the three of them watched the sky in silence.

Diana raised her head and propped it on her elbow. "I don't know if I can fall asleep. It's so . . . obliterating, you know? The feeling of insignificance. Your mind wanders out there and just keeps on going."

Bridget laughed appreciatively. At that moment, Diana reminded her of Carmen in the nicest way, full of philosophy and psychochatter. "Honestly?" Bridget said. "That idea never occurred to me."

Planes are so clean. Carmen liked that. She liked the orderly, corporate smell and the sheer number of wrappers in her snack basket.

She admired the snack itself, the miniature apple. Exactly the right size, shape, and color. Kind of fake, but reassuring at the same time. She tucked it into her bag. She'd save a little order for later.

She'd never been to her dad's apartment—he'd always come to see her instead. But she'd imagined it. Her dad wasn't a slob, but he didn't have that second X chromosome either. There wouldn't be curtains in the windows or dust ruffles on the beds or baking soda in the fridge. There would be a few dust creatures roaming the floor. Maybe not right in the middle of the room, but over by the sofa probably. (There would be a sofa, wouldn't there?) She hoped she would be sleeping on cotton sheets. Knowing her dad, he might have the polyester blend kind. Carmen had polyester issues. She couldn't help it.

Maybe between tennis games and John Woo movies, and whatever things they found to do on a Saturday afternoon, she could take him to Bed Bath & Beyond and get some matching towels and a real teakettle. He would complain about it, but she would make it fun, and afterward he would appreciate her for it. She imagined that maybe he would be sad at the end of the summer and investigate the local high school and ask her, seriously, whether she could ever feel at home in South Carolina.

Carmen glanced down at the row of bumps on her forearm that were making the fine, dark hairs stand up.

She hadn't seen her dad since Christmas. Christmas was always their time. Since the year she was seven and her parents split up, her dad had come every year and stayed at the Embassy Suites in Friendship Heights for four days, and they hung out. They'd go to movies, run on the canal, and return the hilarious Christmas presents she got from his sisters.

Often there were other nights, maybe three or

four during the year, when he would come up to D.C. on business. She knew he took almost any excuse to get up to the Washington area. They always had dinner at a restaurant she picked. She tried to choose places he would like. She always checked his face carefully as he studied the menu and then as he took his first bite. She hardly tasted her own food.

She felt the grinding sound under the plane. Either an engine was falling off, or the wheels were unfolding for landing. It was too cloudy to gauge how close they were to the ground. She pressed her forehead to the cold plastic window. She squinted, wishing for a break in the clouds. She wanted to see the ocean. She wanted to figure out which way was north. She wanted the big picture before she landed.

"Please put your tray in its upright and locked position," a flight attendant chirped to the man sitting next to her in the aisle seat; then she grabbed the remains of Carmen's snack basket. The man next to Carmen was heavy and mostly bald and kept pushing his pleather briefcase into Carmen's shin.

On planes, Bridget always sat next to adorable college guys who asked for her number before they landed. Carmen always got the middle seat between men with fat fingers, class rings, and sales reports.

"Flight attendants, please take your seats," the captain said over the P.A. system. Carmen felt a thrill in the bottom of her stomach. She uncrossed her legs, putting both feet on the ground. She made the sign of the cross like her mother always did at takeoffs and landings. She felt like kind of a faker, but was this really a moment to break superstitions?

Tibby,

You are with me, even though you aren't. I love everything about this trip but being apart and knowing you're sad about being home. I don't feel right being happy knowing that. I feel so weird without you guys. Without you here being Tibby, I'm being a little bit Tibby—doing it badly compared to you, though.

Infinite X's and O's,
Carma

Can you make
yourself love? can
you make yourself be
loved?
—Lena Kaligaris

The first thing was the front door. It was painted the most brilliant, egg-yolk-over-easy shade of yellow. Surrounding it, the house front was painted the brightest possible blue. Who could even imagine such a blue? Lena tipped her face upward to the cloudless afternoon sky. Oh.

In Bethesda, if you painted your house those colors, they'd call you a drug addict. Your neighbors would sue you. They'd arrive with sprayers at nightfall and repaint it beige. Here was color bursting out everywhere against the whitewashed walls.

"Lena, go!" Effie whined, shoving Lena's suitcase forward with her foot.

"Velcome, girls. Velcome home!" Grandma said, clapping her hands. Their grandfather fit the key into the lock and swung open the sun-colored door.

The combination of jet lag, sun, and these strange old people made Lena feel as if she were tripping—hypothetically, of course. She'd never actually tripped on anything, except maybe a bad shrimp from Peking Garden once.

If Lena was glazed and stupefied, Effie without sleep was just plain cranky. Lena always counted on her younger sister to do the blabbering, but Effie was too cranky even for that. So the drive from the tiny island airport had been mostly quiet. Grandma kept turning around in the front seat of their old Fiat saying, "Look at you girls! Oh, Lena, you are a beauty!"

Lena seriously wished she would stop saying that, because it was irritating, and besides, how was cranky Effie supposed to feel?

Grandma's English was good from years of running a restaurant catering to tourists, but Bapi's didn't seem to have benefited in the same way. Lena knew that her grandmother had been the hostess and the beloved public face of the restaurant, charming everyone with tidal waves of affection. Bapi mostly stayed in the back, cooking at first, and then running the business after that.

Lena felt ashamed for not speaking Greek. According to her parents, Greek was her first language as a baby, but she slowly dropped it when she started school. Her parents never even bothered with Effie. It was a whole different alphabet, for God's sake. Now Lena wished she spoke it, just like she wished she were taller and had a singing voice like Sarah McLachlan. She wished it, but she didn't expect it would happen.

"Grandma, I love your door," Lena piped up as she passed through it. The inside of the house was so comparatively dark, Lena felt she might faint. All she could see at first were swirling sunspots.

"Here ve are!" Grandma shouted, clapping again.

Bapi shuttled behind, with two duffel bags and Effie's furry neon-green backpack over both shoulders. It was cute and depressing at the same time.

Grandma threw her arm around Lena and squeezed her tight. On the surface Lena felt glad, but just under the surface it made her feel awkward. She was unsure how to return the gesture.

The house came into focus. It was larger than she expected, with ceramic tile floors and pretty rugs.

"Follow me, girls," Grandma ordered. "I'll show you your rooms and then ve'll have a nice glass of drink, okay?"

Two zombie girls followed her upstairs. The landing was small but gave way to two bedrooms, a bathroom, and a short hallway down which Lena saw two other doors.

Grandma turned into the first door. "This one for beautiful Lena," she said proudly. Lena didn't think so much of the simple room until Grandma threw open the heavy wooden shutters.

"Oh," Lena said, sighing.

Grandma pointed out the window. "Caldera," she announced. "Cauldron, you English say."

"Oh," Lena said again with genuine awe.

Though Lena was still iffy about her grandmother, she fell instantly in love with the Caldera. The water was a darker copy of the sky, teased by the wind just enough to make it glitter and shine. The thin, semicircular island hugged the wide expanse of water. A tiny island popped up in the middle of it.

"Oia is de most beautiful village in Greece," Grandma proclaimed, and Lena couldn't imagine that wasn't true.

Lena looked down at the whitewashed buildings, much like this one, clinging to cliffs jutting down to the water. She hadn't realized before how steep it was, how strange a spot it was to make a home. Santorini was a volcano, after all. She knew from family lore that it was the site of the worst explosion in history and countless tidal waves and earthquakes. The center of the island had literally sunk into the sea, and all that was left was this thin, wobbly crescent of volcanic cliffs and some black ash-tinted sand. The cauldron looked calm and beautiful now, but the true Santorinians liked to remind you it could start bubbling and spewing anytime.

Though Lena had grown up in a flat, sprawling,

grassy suburb where people feared no natural disaster worse than mosquitoes or traffic on the beltway, she'd always known her roots were here. And now, looking out at the water, some deep atavistic memory bubbled up, and it did feel like home.

"My name is Duncan Howe, and I'm your assistant general manager." He pointed with a large, freckly finger to a plastic nameplate. "And now that you've finished orientation, I'd like to welcome you as our newest sales professionals at Wallman's." He spoke with such authority, you would have thought he was talking to a crowd of hundreds rather than two bored, gum-chewing girls.

Tibby imagined a string of drool dangling from the side of her mouth all the way down to the scuffed linoleum squares.

He studied his clipboard. "Now, uh, Tie-by," he began, giving it a long *i*.

"Tibby," she corrected.

"I'd like you to unload inventory in Personal Hygiene, aisle two."

"I thought I was a sales professional," Tibby commented.

"Brianna," he said, ignoring Tibby, "you can start at register four."

Tibby frowned sourly. Brianna got to snap her gum at an empty register because she had uncommonly huge hair and gigantic boobs that even the darts on her smock couldn't accommodate.

"Now don your headsets, and let's get to work," Duncan commanded importantly.

Tibby tried to abort her laugh, so it came out as a combination hack-snort. She slapped her hand over her mouth. Duncan didn't seem to notice.

The good news was, she'd found her star. She'd decided the morning after the vow of the Pants that she was going to record her summer of discontent in a movie—a suckumentary, a pastiche of lameness. Duncan had just won himself a role.

She jammed her headset over her ears and hurried herself to aisle two before she got the boot. On one hand, it would have been excellent to get fired, but on the other, she needed to make money if she was ever going to have a car. She knew from experience that there were few career opportunities for a girl with a pierced nose who couldn't type and was not a "people person."

Tibby went back to the storeroom, where a woman with extraordinarily long fingernails motioned to a very large cardboard box. "Set that up in deodorants and antiperspirants," she instructed in a bored tone. Tibby couldn't look away from the fingernails. They curved like ten scythes. They rivaled the nails of the Indian guy in the *Guinness Book of World Records*. They looked the way Tibby imagined a corpse's fingernails would look after a few years in the ground. She wondered how the woman could pick up a box with those nails. Could she dial a phone? Could she type on the keys on the register? Could she wash her hair? Could a person get fired for having their fingernails too long? Could you maybe get disability? Tibby glanced at her own chewed-up fingernails.

"Any special way?" Tibby asked.

"It's a display," the woman said, as though any moron would know how to set one up. "It's got instructions in the box."

Tibby hefted the box toward aisle two, wondering how the woman's fingernails would look in her movie.

"Your headset is drooping," the woman warned.

When she unpacked the box, Tibby was disheartened to see at least two hundred roll-on antiperspirants and a complicated cardboard contraption. She gaped at the number of arrows and diagrams in the instructions. You needed an engineering degree to put the thing together.

With the help of a little Scotch tape from aisle eight and a wad of gum from her mouth, Tibby at last managed to construct a pyramid of roll-ons with the cardboard head of a sphinx stuck to the top. What did antiperspirant have to do with ancient Egypt? Who knew?

"Tibby!" Duncan marched over importantly.

Tibby looked up from the momentous stack of roll-ons.

"I've paged you four times! We need you at register three!"

Tibby had failed to turn on her drooping headset. She had been too busy making silent fun of it to pay attention when Duncan explained how to use it.

After she had spent one hour at the register and sold exactly two triple-A batteries to a zitty thirteen-year-old, her shift was over.

She took off her smock, turned in her headset, and strode through the doors, to a deafening barrage of bleeps. Duncan jumped in her path with stunning speed for a person on the fat side of fat. "Excuse me, Tibby, could you follow me back inside?"

She could see it all over his face: *We never should have hired the girl with the nose ring.*

He asked to see the contents of her pockets. She didn't have any pockets.

"Your smock?" he pressed.

"Oh." She pulled the rumpled smock from under her arm. From the pocket she pulled her wallet and . . . a partly used roll of Scotch tape. "Oh, that," Tibby said. "Right. See, I just used it for the . . ."

Duncan's face took on a resigned "I've heard all the excuses under the sun" expression. "Look, Tibby. We have a second-chance policy here at Wallman's, so we'll let this go. But be warned: I am forced to suspend your best-employee benefits, namely a fifteen percent We-Are-Wallman's discount on all items."

After that Duncan carefully noted that the price of the Scotch tape be deducted from her first day's pay. Then he disappeared for a moment and came back with a see-through plastic bag with two handles. "Could you please keep your possessions in this from now on?" he asked.

Dear Carmen,

I guess when you have close blood relatives you've never met, you can't help but kind of idealize them in your mind. Like how adopted kids always believe their birth father was a professor and their birth mother was a model?

I guess with my grandparents it was kind of the same thing. My parents always said I was beautiful just like Grandma. So somehow all these years I pictured Grandma as Cindy Crawford or something. Grandma is not Cindy Crawford. She is old. She has a bad perm and an old-lady velour sweat suit, and horny-looking toenails sticking out of her pink, flat sandals. She's pretty ordinary, you know?

Bapi, the legendary businessman of the Kaligaris family, I pictured as being at least six feet two. He's not. He's teeny. Maybe my height. He wears thick brown double-knit trousers even though it's over a million degrees here, and a white shirt with a zipper at the collar. His shoes are cream-colored vinyl. He's sort of moldy and speckled in that old-man way. He's very shy.

I feel like I should just love them right away. But how do you do that? You can't make yourself love someone, can you?

I'm taking good care of the Pants. And I miss you. I know you won't judge me harshly for being a brat, 'cause you always think better of me than I deserve.

Love you lots.
Lena

There is no such
thing as fun for the
whole family.
—Jerry Seinfeld

The sunset was too beautiful. It almost made Lena feel panicked because she couldn't save it. The blobs of paint on her palette, usually inspiring, looked hopelessly drab. The sunset burned with a billion watts of light. There was no light in her paint. She put her palette and her carefully prepared panel on top of the wardrobe so she didn't have to look at them.

She perched on her windowsill, gazing at the lurid sun soaking into the Caldera, trying to appreciate it even though she couldn't have it. Why did she always feel she had to *do* something in the face of beauty?

She heard the bustle of a feast being prepared downstairs. Grandma and Bapi were celebrating their arrival with a big meal and a bunch of neighbors. Her grandparents had sold their restaurant two years ago, but they hadn't lost their love for food, Lena guessed. Spicy, rich smells, one after another, floated upstairs into Lena's room, mixing together for a preview of the full meal.

"Lena! Almost ready!" Grandma shouted from the kitchen. "You dress and come down!"

Lena threw her suitcase and her duffel bag on the bed, so she could keep her eyes on the window. Getting dressed was rarely exciting to her. She wore practical clothes, "stodgy, dull, and pathetic," according to her friends. She didn't like people having more reasons to look at her, to think that how she looked made them know her. She'd been the show pony too often as a child.

Tonight, though, there was a little carbonation in the bottom of her stomach. Carefully she dug under layers of clothes to find the Pants. They felt a little heavier than they deserved. She held her breath as she unfolded them, letting loose a thousand wishes into the air. This was the beginning of their history, their life as the Traveling Pants. As she pulled them on she felt the enormity of making them count. She momentarily tried to picture herself having big moments in the Pants. For some reason, she couldn't shake the vision of Effie wearing them instead.

She stuck her feet into a pair of beat-up brown loafers and headed downstairs.

"I made a meatball," Effie declared proudly from the kitchen.

"Keftedes," Grandma clarified over her shoulder, equally proud. "Effie is a Kaligaris. She likes to cook and she likes to eat!" She gave Effie a hug to confirm what a good thing this was.

Lena smiled and went into the kitchen to praise and investigate.

She and Effie were already putting on their turtle-and-hare show. Everyone paid lots of attention to Lena at first, because she was striking to look at, but within a few hours or days, they always fully committed their attentions to exuberant, affectionate Effie. Lena felt Effie deserved it. Lena was an introvert. She knew she had trouble connecting with people. She always felt like her looks were fake bait, seeming to offer a bridge to people, which she couldn't easily cross.

Grandma cast a look at her outfit. "You are wearing that to our party?"

"I was thinking so. Should I wear something fancier?" Lena asked.

"Well . . ." Grandma did not look particularly stern or judgmental. She looked more mischievous, like she had a secret she wanted you to ask her about. "It isn't a fancy party, but . . ."

"Should I change too?" Effie asked. Her shirt was dusty with breadcrumbs.

Grandma was about as good at keeping her secrets as Effie was. She looked at Lena conspiratorially. "You see, there is a boy, he's like a grandson to Bapi and me. He's a *nice* boy. . . ." She winked.

Lena tried to freeze the pleasant look on her face. Was her grandmother seriously trying to set her up with a guy less than six hours after she'd arrived? Lena *hated* being set up.

Effie looked pained on her behalf.

"His name is Kostos," Grandma plowed on, oblivious. "He is the grandson of our dear friends and neighbors."

Studying her grandmother's face, Lena had a strong suspicion Grandma hadn't just cooked up this idea in the last hour. She suspected Grandma had been plotting something for a long time. She knew arranged marriages were still popular among Greek parents, particularly in the islands, but God!

Effie laughed awkwardly. "Um, Grandma? Boys love Lena, but Lena is very hard on boys."

Lena's eyebrows shot up. "Effie! Thanks a lot!"

Effie shrugged sweetly. "It's true."

"Lena hasn't met Kostos," Grandma said confidently. "Everyone loves Kostos."

"Sweetheart!"

Carmen's heart took off faster than her feet at the sight of her dad waving his arms at her from behind the Plexiglas half wall delineating gate forty-two. She felt like a cliché, running like that, but she loved it anyway.

"Hey, Dad!" she called, throwing herself at him. She savored that word. Most kids got to use it constantly, thoughtlessly. For her it lay unused, stashed away so many months of the year.

He held her tightly for just long enough. He let go, and she looked up at him. She loved how tall he was. He took her shoulder bag and tossed it over his own shoulder even though it was light. She smiled at the way he looked with her turquoise sequined bag.

"Hi, baby!" he said happily, putting his free arm around her shoulder. "How was the flight?" he asked, steering her toward the baggage claim area.

"Perfect," she said. It was always awkward, their uneven strides with his arm around her shoulders, but she liked it too much to mind. Let other girls who saw their fathers every day complain. She saw hers only a few times a year.

"You look beautiful, bun," he said easily. "You grew taller, I think." He put his hand on the top of her head.

"I did," she said proudly, always pleased at the idea that her height made her like him. "I'm five six and a half," she reported. "Almost five seven."

"Wow," he said from his height of six foot two. "Wow. How is your mother?"

He always asked that dutiful question within the first five minutes.

"She's fine," Carmen always answered, knowing her dad didn't want a full answer. Year after year, Carmen's mother continued to be rabidly curious about her dad, but her dad only asked about her mom to be polite.

Noiseless drops of guilt colored Carmen's pleasure. She was almost five seven, but her mother wasn't even five feet tall. Her dad called her bun and said she was beautiful, but he didn't care about her mom anymore.

"How are your buddies?" he asked, as they squished together onto the escalator, his arm still around her shoulders.

He knew how it was with her and Tibby and Lena and Bridget. He always remembered the details of her friends' lives from the last time he talked to her.

"It's a weird summer for us," she answered. "It's our first summer apart. Lena's in Greece with her grandparents; Bridget's at soccer camp in Baja California. Tibby's home alone."

"And you're here all summer," he said, with an almost undetectable question in his eyes.

"I'm so glad to be here," she said, her answer loud and clear. "I can't wait. It's just weird, you know? I mean, not weird in a bad way. Weird in a good way. It'll be good for us to branch out a little. You know how we get." She was babbling, she realized. She hated for her dad to be uncertain.

He pointed to a conveyor belt, zipping luggage around in a circle. "I think this is for your flight."

She remembered the time in Washington, when he held both her hands over her head while she rode the carousel halfway around. Then a guard yelled at them, and he pulled her off.

"It's a big black one with wheels. It looks like everybody else's," she said. It was strange that he'd never seen her suitcase before. She'd never seen him without his.

"There!" she said suddenly, and he pounced. He pulled her suitcase off the conveyor belt as though his life had prepared him for that job alone. The turquoise sequins on her shoulder bag sparkled.

He carried the big suitcase instead of rolling it. "Great! Let's go." He pointed them in the direction of the parking lot.

"Do you still have your Saab?" she asked. Cars were one of the interests they had in common.

"No. I traded it in this past spring for a station wagon."

"Really?" She couldn't quite make sense of that one. "Do you like it?"

"It does the job," he said, steering them right to it. It was a beige Volvo. His Saab had been red. "And here we go." He opened her door for her and settled her in with her bag before loading her suitcase into the back. Where did dads learn these things? Why didn't they teach them to their sons?

"How did school finish up?" he asked her as he maneuvered out of the parking lot.

"Really good," she answered. She always looked forward to giving him the rundown. "I got As in math, bio, English, French, and an A minus in world history." Her mother thought she worried about school too much. To her dad, grades mattered.

"Bun, that's fabulous. And sophomore year is an important year."

She knew he wanted her to go to Williams, just like he had, and he knew she wanted to too, even though they didn't say it to each other out loud.

"What about tennis?" he asked.

Most people she knew hated these kinds of dad questions, but Carmen worked all year for them. "Bridget and I played first doubles. We only lost one match."

She wouldn't bother to tell him that she got an F in pottery—it wouldn't go on her transcript—or that the boy she'd crushed on all year asked Lena to the prom or that she'd made her mother cry on Easter Sunday. These conversations were about her victories.

"I got a court for us on Saturday," he told her, accelerating onto a highway.

Carmen studied the scenery. There were motels and strip developments like there were around almost every airport, but the air smelled heavier and saltier here. She studied her dad's face. He had a tan already. It made his blue eyes stand out. She always wished she'd gotten his eyes rather than her mother's brown ones. His hair looked recently cut, and his shirt was crisp and neatly cuffed. She wondered if he'd gotten a raise or something.

"I can't wait to see your place," she said.

"Yeah," he said absently, glancing into the rearview mirror before he changed lanes.

"Isn't it pretty amazing that I've never been here before?" she asked.

He concentrated on the driving. "You know, bun, it's not that I haven't wanted you to come long before this. I just wanted to get settled better before I brought you here." There was a trace of apology in his eyes when he glanced at her.

She didn't mean to make him uncomfortable. "Dad, I don't care if you're settled. Don't worry about that. We'll have a great time. Who cares about settled?"

He exited the highway. "I couldn't see bringing you into my hectic life. Working so much, living alone in a one-bedroom apartment. Eating every meal out."

She couldn't talk fast enough. "I can't wait for that. I love eating out. I'm sick of being settled." She meant it. This was the summer of Carmen and Al.

He didn't say anything as they drove along small wooded suburban streets with big Victorian houses rising on either side. Raindrops burst on the windshield. The sky grew so dark it felt almost like nighttime. He slowed down and stopped in front of a cream-colored Victorian with green-gray shutters and a wraparound porch.

"Where's this?" Carmen asked.

Her dad cut the engine and turned to her. "This is home." His eyes were distant and a little mysterious. He didn't seem to want to take on the open surprise in hers.

"That house? Up there? I thought you lived in an apartment downtown."

"I moved. Just last month."

"You did? Why didn't you tell me on the phone?"

"Because . . . there's a lot of big stuff, bun. Stuff I wanted to say in person," he answered.

She wasn't sure how she felt about big stuff. She turned in her seat. "So? Are you going to tell me?" Carmen was never graceful about surprises.

"Let's go inside, okay?"

He opened his door and hurried around to her side before she echoed his okay. He didn't get her suitcase. He held his coat over both their heads as they climbed stone steps up to the house.

He took her arm in his. "Careful. These steps get slippery when it rains," he said, leading her up the painted wood steps of the front porch. It was as though he'd lived here forever.

Carmen's heart was thumping. She had no idea where they were or what to expect. She felt the shape of the apple in her bag.

Her dad pushed open the door without knocking. "Here we are!" he called.

Carmen realized she was holding her breath. Who would be here?

Within seconds a woman came into the room with a girl who appeared to be about Carmen's age. Carmen stood baffled and stiff as the woman and then the girl each hugged her. They were quickly followed by a tall young man, about eighteen, Carmen guessed. He was blond and broad, like an athlete. She was thankful that he didn't hug her.

"Lydia, Krista, Paul, this is my daughter, Carmen," her dad said. Her name sounded weird in his voice. He always called her sweetheart or baby or bun. He never called her Carmen. She thought that was because it was her Puerto Rican grandmother's name, and Carmen Sr. had sent him several nasty letters after the divorce. Her father's mother was dead. Her name was Mary.

They all stared at her expectantly, smiling. She had no idea what to say or do.

"Carmen, this is Lydia." Pause, pause, pause. "My fiancée. And Krista and Paul, her children."

Carmen closed her eyes and opened them again. The soft lights around the room made floaty spots in her vision. "When did you get a fiancée?" she asked in a near whisper. She knew it wasn't the most polite phrasing.

Her father laughed. "April twenty-fourth, to be exact," he said. "I moved in mid-May."

"And you're getting married?" She knew that was an incredibly stupid thing to say.

"In August," he said. "The nineteenth."

"Oh," she said.

"Quite amazing, isn't it?" he asked.

"Amazing," she echoed faintly, though her tone wasn't the same as his.

Lydia took one of her hands. Carmen felt as though it no longer belonged to her body. "Carmen, we are *so* thrilled to have you this summer. Why don't you come inside and relax? Would you like a soda or a cup of tea? Albert will show you your room so you can get settled."

Albert? Who ever called her father Albert? And what was all this about getting settled? What was she doing in this house? This wasn't where she was spending her summer.

"Carmen?" her dad said. "Soda? Tea?"

Carmen just turned to him, wide-eyed, not quite hearing. She nodded.

"Which? Both?" her dad pressed.

She looked around the kitchen. Stainless steel appliances like rich people had. There was an oriental carpet on the floor. Who had an oriental carpet in their kitchen? There was an old-fashioned southern-style fan overhead. It turned slowly. She could hear the rain beating against the window.

"Carmen? Carmen?" Her dad was trying to mask his impatience.

"Sorry," she murmured. She realized Lydia was poised at the cupboard, waiting for orders. "Nothing for me. Could you please tell me where I should put my stuff?"

Her dad looked pained. Did he see how distressed she was? Did he notice? Then the look vanished. "Yes. Come with me. I'll show you your room, then I'll bring your suitcase right up."

She followed him up carpeted stairs, past three bedrooms, to a bedroom facing the backyard with a thick peach-colored carpet, antique furniture, and two Kleenex boxes cased in Lucite—one on the bureau and one on the night table. It had curtains and a dust ruffle all right. And she would bet one billion dollars there was at least one box of baking soda in the refrigerator downstairs. "Is this the guest room?" she asked.

"Yes," he answered, not understanding what she meant. "You get settled," he said, using that idiotic word again. "I'll bring your suitcase up."

He started for the door. "Hey, Dad?"

He turned. He looked wary.

"It's just that . . ." She trailed off. She wanted to

tell him it was pretty inconsiderate not to give her any warning. It was pretty harsh walking into this house full of strangers without any preparation.

In his eyes was a plea. She felt it more than she saw it. He just wanted it to be nice between them.

"Nothing," she said faintly.

She watched him go, realizing she was like him in another way. When she was with him, she didn't like to say the hard things.

Dear Bee,

The summer of Carmen and Al didn't survive past the trip from the airport. My dad is now Albert and is marrying Lydia and lives in a house full of kleenex boxes and is playing father to two blond people. Forget about all the things I imagined. I'm a guest in the guest room of a family that will never be mine.

Sorry, Bee. I'm being self-absorbed again. I know I'm a big baby, but my heart is rotting. I hate surprises.

Love you and miss you,
Carmen

66

Love is like war:
easy to begin, hard
to end.

—Proverb

"Lena."

Lena looked up from her journal as Effie appeared in her doorway. Effie scrambled in and sat on her bed. "People are here, you know. The party's starting."

Lena had heard voices downstairs, but she was prepared to pretend she hadn't.

"*He's* here," Effie continued meaningfully.

"He?"

"Kostos."

"So?"

Effie got a look on her face. "Lena, I'm not kidding; you've got to see him."

"Why?"

Effie leaned forward on her elbows. "I know you'd think he'd be this little . . . Grandma's boy, but Lena, he is . . . he is . . ." When Effie got excited she didn't finish her sentences.

"He's what?"

"He's . . ."

Lena raised an eyebrow.

"Stupendous," Effie declared.

Lena was naturally a little curious, but she wouldn't admit it. "Ef, I didn't come to Greece to find a boyfriend."

"Can I have him?"

Lena smiled for real. "Effie, *yes*. Does it matter that you already have a boyfriend?"

"It did until I saw Kostos."

"He's that great, huh?"

"You'll see."

Lena stood. "So let's go." It was handy to have Kostos built up so much. When she saw him he would certainly be disappointing.

Effie paused. "You told Grandma you were coming up to change."

"Oh, yeah." Lena rifled through her bag. It was cool now that the sun had set. She put on a brown turtleneck—her least sexy piece of clothing—and pulled her hair back in a severe ponytail. Still, the Pants were the Pants.

"You know, those pants do seem kind of magical," Effie enthused. "They look great on you. Like, even better than usual."

"Thanks," Lena said. "Let's go."

"Wheeee," Effie said excitedly.

So Kostos wasn't disappointing. He was tall. He looked more like a man than a boy; he looked at least eighteen. He was good-looking enough to make Lena suspicious.

Granted, Lena was suspicious of many things. But she had earned her suspicions about boys. Lena knew boys: They never looked beyond your looks. They pretended to be your friend to get you to trust them, and as soon as you trusted them, they went in for the grope. They pretended to want to work on a history project or volunteer on your blood drive committee to get your attention. But as soon as they got it through their skulls that you didn't want to go out with them, they suddenly weren't interested in time lines or dire blood shortages. Worst of all, on occasion they even went out with one of your best friends to get close to you, and broke that same best friend's heart when the truth came out. Lena preferred plain guys to cute ones, but even the plain ones disappointed her.

She personally thought that the only reason most girls put up with most boys at all was because they needed reassurance that they were pretty. That was one thing, maybe the only thing, Lena knew about herself without reassurance.

Lena's friends called her Aphrodite, the goddess of love and beauty. The beauty part was more or less on target, but the love part was a joke. Lena was not a romantic.

"Lena, this is Kostos," Grandma said. Lena could tell Grandma was trying to be cool, but she was just about blowing a gasket with excitement.

"Kostos, this is my granddaughter Lena," Grandma said with a flourish, as though she were presenting a game show contestant with his new red car.

Lena stuck her hand out stiffly and shook his, heading off any spontaneous Greek cheek-kissing.

He studied her face while he shook her hand. She could tell he was trying to hold her eyes for a moment, but she looked down.

"Kostos is going to university in London in the fall," Grandma bragged, as though he were hers. "He tried out with the national football team," she added. "We are all so proud of him."

Now Kostos was the one looking down. "Valia brags more than my own grandmother," he mumbled.

Lena noted that his English was accented but sure.

"But this summer, Kostos is helping his *bapi*," Grandma announced, and literally brushed a tear from the corner of her eye. "Bapi Dounas had a problem with his . . ." Grandma patted her hand over her heart. "Kostos changed his summer plans to stay home and help."

Now Kostos looked genuinely uncomfortable. Lena felt sudden sympathy for him. "Valia, Bapi is strong as ever. I always like to work at the forge."

Lena knew he was lying, and she liked him for it. Then she had a better idea.

"Kostos, have you met my sister, Effie, yet?" Effie had been bobbing around nearby the whole time, so it wasn't hard to find her elbow and pull her over.

Kostos smiled. "You look like sisters," he said, and Lena wanted to hug him for it. For some reason, people always paid more attention to their differences than their similarities. Maybe it took a Greek to see it. "Who's older?" he asked.

"I'm older, but Effie's nicer," Lena said.

"Oh, please," Grandma said, practically snorting.

"Just a year older," Effie chimed in. "Fifteen months, actually."

"I see," Kostos answered.

"She's only fourteen," Grandma felt the need to point out. "Lena will be sixteen at the end of the summer."

"Do you have brothers or sisters?" Effie, the eager subject-changer, asked.

Kostos's face became subtly guarded. "No . . . just me."

"Oh," both girls said. Judging from Kostos's expression, Lena could tell there was more to the story than that, and she silently prayed Effie wouldn't ask any more about it. She didn't want to get into intimacies here.

"Kostos . . . uh . . . plays soccer," Lena tossed in, just to be sure.

"Plays soccer?" Grandma practically shouted as though scandalized. "He is a champion! He's a hero in Oia!"

Kostos laughed, so Lena and Effie did too.

"You young people. You talk," Grandma ordered, and she vanished.

Lena decided this could be a good opportunity to give Kostos and Effie a moment. "I'm going to get more food," she said.

Later, she sat on the single chair outside the front door eating delicious stuffed grape leaves called *dolmades*, and olives. As many thousands of times as she'd eaten Greek food back in Maryland, it had never tasted precisely like this.

Kostos peered out the door. "There you are," he said. "You like to sit alone?"

She nodded. She'd chosen this spot mostly for its one chair.

"I see." He was very, very handsome. His hair was dark and wavy, and his eyes were yellow-green. There was a slight bump on the bridge of his nose.

That means you should go away, she urged him silently.

Kostos walked into the passageway that led past her grandparents' home and wound up the cliff. He pointed downhill. "That's my house," he said, pointing to a similar structure about five doors down. It had a wrought-iron balcony on the second floor painted a vibrant green and holding back an avalanche of flowers.

"Oh. Long walk," she said.

He smiled.

She was about to ask whether he lived with his grandparents, but then she realized that would be inviting a conversation.

He leaned against the whitewashed wall of the passageway. So much for the notion that Greek men were short.

"Would you like to take a walk with me?" he asked. "I want to show you Ammoudi, the little village at the bottom of the cliff."

"No thanks," she said. She didn't even make an excuse. She had learned long ago that boys took excuses as further reasons to ask you out.

He studied her face a moment, openly disappointed. "Maybe another time," he said.

She wanted him to go back inside and ask Effie to see Ammoudi, but instead he walked slowly down the hill and into his house.

I'm sorry you asked me out, she told him silently. *Otherwise maybe I could have liked you.*

There were guys at soccer camp, as it turned out. There was one guy. No, there was more than one guy, but for Bridget, at that moment, there was one guy.

He was a coach, it appeared. He was on the other side of the field, consulting with Connie. He had dark straight hair and skin several shades darker than hers. He looked Hispanic, maybe. He had the graceful build of a midfielder. Even from here, his face looked complicated for a soccer coach. He was beautiful.

"It's not polite to stare."

Bridget turned and smiled at Ollie. "I can't help myself."

Ollie nodded. "He is every kind of hot."

"Do you know him?" Bridget asked.

"From last year," Ollie explained. "He was assistant coach of my team. We drooled all summer."

"What's his name?"

"Eric Richman. He's from L.A. He plays at Columbia. I guess he'll probably be a sophmore this year."

So he was older, but not *that* much older.

"Don't get your hopes up," Ollie said, reading her mind. "The camp has a big antifraternizing policy, obviously. He follows it, though a lot of people have tried to get him not to."

"Let's gather!" Connie was shouting across the milling clumps of girls.

Bridget pulled her hair out of the elastic. It fell

around her shoulders, seeming to capture far more than its fair share of sunlight. She wandered over to where Connie had gathered with the other coaches.

"I'm going to read out the teams," Connie told the assembled group. Like many other longtime coaches, she had a voice loud as a bullhorn when it was necessary. "This is a big deal, okay? You stick with your team for two months, from the first scrimmages to the Coyote Cup at the end of the summer, okay? Know your team. Love your team." She looked around at the collection of faces. "You all know great soccer isn't about great players. It's about great teams."

The crowd let out a little cheer. Bridget loved these pep talks. She knew they were corny, but they always worked on her. She imagined Tibby rolling her eyes.

"Before I read out the teams, let me introduce the rest of the staff—coaches, assistant coaches, and trainers." Connie went through all of them, giving their names and a little bit about their backgrounds, and finishing with Eric. Did Eric get an extraloud cheer, or did Bridget imagine it?

Connie explained there were six teams, distinct from the cabin assignments. Each team had its own color, and they would each be given team shirts when their names were called. For the moment they'd be called one through six, and then the teams could have the honor of naming themselves. Blah blah. Connie assigned each of the six teams a head coach, an assistant, and a trainer. Eric was with team four.

Please let me be on his team, Bridget silently begged.

Connie consulted the ubiquitous clipboard.

"Aaron, Susanna, team five."

Time to calm down; the list was alphabetical. Bridget found herself hating every girl chosen for team four.

At last, the *V*s. "Vreeland, Bridget, team three."

She was disappointed. But when she strode forward to collect her three identical green T-shirts, she was gratified to see that Eric, whatever else he was, was not immune to her hair.

Carma,

Leave it to me to fall in love at an all-girls' camp. I haven't even spoken to him. His name is Eric. He is beyooootiful. I want him.

I wish you could see him. You would love him. But you can't have him. He's mine! Mine!

I'm insane. I'm going swimming. This is a very romantic place.

—Bee

Rule #1: The customer is always right.
Rule #2: If the customer is wrong, please refer to rule #1.
—Duncan Howe

I'm dying a slow death at Wallman's, Tibby decided the next afternoon under the whirring fluorescent lights. This job probably wouldn't cause death any sooner than the normal time. But it would be very painful.

Why don't stores like this ever have any windows? she wondered. Did they imagine one glimpse of sunshine might cause their caged, pasty employees to bolt?

Today she was back in aisle two, this time restocking geriatric diapers. What was it about her and personal hygiene? Last night her mother had asked her to use her special discount to get diapers for her brother and sister. She didn't confess that she'd already lost her discount.

As she stacked packages of Depends, her body and brain functions seemed to slow to their lowest setting. She could imagine her brainwaves flat-lining on one of those hospital machines. Just dying here at Wallman's.

Suddenly she heard a crash, and she snapped her head around. In fascination she watched her entire pyramid of roll-on antiperspirants collapse under the weight of a falling girl. The falling girl didn't catch herself, as Tibby expected, but dropped right to the ground, her head making a hollow *thwonk* on the linoleum.

Oh, God, Tibby thought, running over to the girl. Tibby had the sensation that she was watching it happen on TV rather than actually experiencing it. Antiperspirant rolled in all directions. The girl was maybe ten or so. Her eyes were closed. Her blond hair fanned out over the floor. Was she dead? Tibby wondered in a panic. She remembered her headset. "Hello! Hello!" she shouted into it, pressing various buttons, wishing she knew how to work it.

She sprinted toward the front checkout. "Emergency! There's an emergency in aisle two! Call 911!" she ordered. It was rare she spoke so many words in a row without a hint of sarcasm. "A girl is lying unconscious in aisle two!"

Satisfied that Brianna was making the call, Tibby ran back to the girl. She was still lying there, not moving. Tibby took her hand. She searched for a pulse, feeling like she'd suddenly landed on an emergency room show. A pulse was pulsing away.

She reached for the girl's wallet in her purse, then she stopped herself. Weren't you not supposed to touch anything until the police got there? Or, no, that was if it was a murder. She was mixing up her cop shows and her doctor shows. She went ahead and got the wallet. Whoever this girl's parents were would certainly want to know that she was lying unconscious in the middle of Wallman's.

There was a library card. A handy horoscope card cut out from a magazine. Some girl's toothy school picture with the name Maddie and a lot of Xs and Os on the back. Four one-dollar bills. How completely useless. It was just the kind of stuff Tibby had carried in her wallet when she was that age.

At that moment three EMS guys carrying a stretcher stormed the aisle. Two of them started poking at the girl, and the other studied a silver medical bracelet encircling her left wrist. Tibby hadn't thought about checking the girl's wrist.

The third guy had questions for Tibby. "So what happened?" he asked. "Did you see?"

"Not exactly," Tibby said. "I heard a noise, and I turned around and I saw her crashing into the display there. She hit her head on the floor. I guess she fainted."

The EMS guy was no longer focused on Tibby's face, but on the wallet she held in her hands. "What's that?" he asked.

"Oh, uh, her wallet."

"You took her wallet?"

Tibby's eyes opened wide. She suddenly realized how it looked. "I mean, I was just—"

"Why don't you go ahead and give that back to me," the man said slowly. Was he treating her like a criminal, or was she being paranoid?

Tibby didn't feel like ridiculing him with her famous mouth. She felt like crying. "I wanted to find her phone number," she explained, shoving the wallet at him. "I wanted to tell her parents what was going on."

The man's eyes softened. "Why don't you just sit tight for a second while we get her into the ambulance. The hospital will take care of contacting her parents."

Tibby clutched the wallet and followed the men and the stretcher outside. In seconds they'd loaded the girl up. Tibby saw by the stain on the girl's jeans and the wetness left behind that she'd peed on herself. Tibby quickly turned her head, as she always did when she saw a stranger crying. Fainting and whacking your head seemed okay to witness, but this felt like too much information.

"Can I come along?" Tibby didn't know why she'd asked. Except that she was worried the girl would wake up and only see scary EMS guys. They made room so that Tibby could sit close to the girl. She reached out and held the girl's hand. Again, she wasn't sure why, except that she had a feeling that if she were zooming down Old Georgetown Road in an ambulance, she would want somebody to be holding her hand.

At the intersection of Wisconsin and Bradley, the girl came to. She looked around blinking, confused. She squeezed Tibby's hand, then looked to see whose hand it was. When she saw Tibby, she looked bewildered and then skeptical. Wide-eyed, the girl took in Tibby's "Hi, I'm Tibby!" name tag and her green smock. Then she turned to the EMS guy sitting on her other side.

"Why is the girl from Wallman's holding my hand?" she asked.

There was a knock. Carmen glanced at the door and sat up on the rug. Her suitcase was open, but she hadn't put anything away. "Yes?"

"Could I come in?"

She was pretty sure it was Krista.

No, you can't. "Uh, yeah."

The door opened tentatively. "Carmen? It's, um, dinnertime? Are you ready to come down?"

Only Krista's head came through the doorway. Carmen could smell her lip gloss. She suspected Krista was an uptalker. Even declarative statements came out as questions.

"I'll be down in a minute," Carmen said.

Krista retreated and closed the door.

Carmen stretched back out on her floor for a minute. How did she get here? How had this happened? She pictured the alternate-universe Carmen, who was polishing off a burger with her dad at a downtown restaurant, before challenging him to a game of pool. She was jealous of that Carmen.

Carmen trudged downstairs and took her place at the elaborately set table. Multiple forks were fine at a restaurant, but in somebody's own dining room? There were matching white covered dishes that turned out to contain all kinds of homemade food. Lamb chops, roasted potatoes, sautéed zucchini and red peppers, carrot salad, warm bread. Carmen jumped when she felt Krista's hand reaching for hers. She yanked it away without thinking.

Krista's cheeks flushed. "Sorry," she murmured. "We hold hands for grace."

She looked at her father. He was happily holding Paul's hand on one side and reaching for hers on the other. *That's what they do. What do we do?* she felt like asking her father. *Aren't we supposed to be a family too?* She submitted to hand-holding and an unfamiliar grace. Her father was the one who'd refused to convert to Catholicism to please Carmen's maternal grandparents. Now he was Mr. Grace?

Carmen thought forlornly of her mom. She and

her mom said grace now, but they hadn't when her dad still lived with them.

She stared at Lydia. What kind of power did this woman have?

"Lydia, this is fabulous," her father said.

"It's great," Krista chimed in.

Carmen felt her father's eyes on her. She was supposed to say something. She just sat there and chewed.

Paul was quiet. He looked at Carmen, then looked down.

Rain slapped against the window. Silverware scraped and teeth chewed.

"Well, Carmen," Krista ventured. "You don't look at all like I was imagining?"

Carmen swallowed a big bite without chewing. This didn't help. She cleared her throat. "You mean, I look Puerto Rican?" She leveled Krista with a stare.

Krista tittered and then backtracked. "No, I just meant . . . you know . . . you have, like, dark eyes and dark wavy hair?"

And dark skin and a big butt? Carmen felt like adding. "Right," Carmen said. "I look Puerto Rican, like my mother. My mother is Puerto Rican. As in Hispanic. My dad might not have mentioned that."

Krista's voice grew so quiet, Carmen wasn't even sure she was still talking. "I'm not sure if he . . ." Krista trailed off till she was just mouthing words at her plate.

"Carmen has my height and my talent for math," her dad piped up. It was lame, but Carmen appreciated it anyway.

Lydia nodded earnestly. Paul still didn't say anything.

"So, Carmen." Lydia placed her fork on her plate. "Your father tells me you are a wonderful tennis player."

Carmen's mouth happened to be completely full at that moment. It seemed to take about five long minutes to chew and swallow. "I'm okay," was the big payoff to all that chewing.

Carmen knew she was being stingy with her little answers. She could have expanded or asked a question back. But she was angry. She was so angry she didn't understand herself. She didn't want Lydia's food to taste good. She didn't want her dad to enjoy it so much. She didn't want Krista to look like a little doll in her lavender cardigan. She wanted Paul to actually say something and not just sit there thinking she was a stupid lunatic. She hated these people. She didn't want to be here. Suddenly she felt dizzy. She felt panic cramping her stomach. Her heart was knocking around unsteadily.

She stood up. "Can I call Mom?" she asked her dad.

"Of course," he said, getting up too. "Why don't you use the phone in the guest room?"

She left the table without another word and ran upstairs.

"Mamaaa," she sobbed into the phone a minute later. Every day since the end of school, she'd pushed her mother away little by little, anticipating her summer with her dad. Now she needed her mother, and she needed her mother to forget about all those times.

"What is it, baby?"

"Daddy's getting married. He's got a whole family now. He's got a wife and two blond kids and this fancy house. What am I doing here?"

"Oh, Carmen. My gosh. He's getting married, is he? Who is she?"

Her mom couldn't help letting a little of her own curiosity creep through her concern.

"Yes. In August. Her name is Lydia."

"Lydia who?"

"I don't even know." Carmen cast herself upon the floral bedspread.

Her mother sighed. "What are the kids like?"

"I don't know. Blond. Quiet."

"How old?"

Carmen didn't feel like answering questions. She felt like getting babied and pitied. "Teenagers. The boy is older than me. I really don't know exactly."

"Well, he should have told you before you went down there."

Carmen could detect the edge of anger in her mother's voice. But she didn't want to deal with it right now.

"It's fine, Mom. He said he wanted to tell me in person. It's just . . . I don't even feel like being here anymore."

"Oh, honey, you're disappointed not to have your daddy to yourself."

When it was put like that, Carmen couldn't find the appropriate space for her indignation.

"It's not that," she wailed. "They're so . . ."

"What?"

"I don't like them." Carmen's anger made her inarticulate.

"Why not?"

"I just don't. They don't like me either."

"How can you tell?" her mom asked.

"I just can," Carmen said sullenly, loathing herself for being such a baby.

"Are you mad at these strangers, or are you mad at your dad?"

"I'm not mad at Dad," Carmen said quickly without taking even a moment to consider it. It wasn't his fault he'd fallen for a woman with zombies for children and a guest room straight out of a Holiday Inn.

She said good-bye to her mother and promised to call the next day. Then she rolled over and cried for reasons she didn't quite understand.

Some sane part of her brain told her she should feel happy for her dad. He'd met a woman he loved enough to marry. He had this whole life now. It was obviously what he wanted. She knew she should want for him what he wanted for himself.

But still she hated them. And so she hated herself for hating them.

Slowly Bridget waded into the warm water. A thousand triggerfish darted around her ankles.

"I want Eric," she told Diana, who was on team four. "Will you trade places with me?" It wasn't the first time she'd proposed this.

Diana laughed at her. "Do you think they'd notice?"

"He's leading a run at five," Emily said.

Bridget looked at her watch. "Shit, that's in five minutes."

"You're not seriously going to go," Diana said.

Bridget was already out of the water. "Yeah, I am."

"It's six miles," Emily said.

The truth was Bridget hadn't run even one mile in over two months. "Where are they meeting up?"

"By the equipment shed," Emily said, wading deeper into the water.

"See you all," Bridget called over her shoulder.

In the cabin, she yanked on a pair of shorts over her bikini bottoms and traded her top for a sports bra. She pulled on socks and her running shoes. It was too hot to worry about whether running in just the bra was acceptable.

The group had already started off. Bridget had to chase them down a dirt path. She should have taken a minute to stretch.

There were about fifteen of them. Bridget hung back for the first mile or so until she found her stride. Her legs were long, and she carried no extra weight. It made her a naturally good runner, even when she was out of practice.

She pulled up with the middle of the pack. Eric noticed her. She pulled up closer to him. "Hi. I'm Bridget," she said.

"Bridget?" He let her catch up with him.

"Most people call me Bee, though."

"Bee? As in bumble?"

She nodded and smiled.

"I'm Eric," he offered.

"I know," she said.

He turned to face the group. "We're doing seven-minute miles today. I'm assuming we have serious runners in this group. If you get tired, just fall back to your own pace. I don't expect everybody to finish with me."

Jesus. Seven-minute miles. The path led uphill. She kicked up dust from the dry ground. Over the hills the land flattened out again. They ran along a riverbed, which carried just a trickle in the dry season.

She was sweating, but her breathing was in check. She stayed up with Eric. "I hear you're from L.A.," she said. Some people liked to talk when they ran. Some people hated it. She was interested to test out which type he was.

"Yeah," he said.

She had just cast him as a type two when he opened his mouth again. "I've spent a lot of time here, though."

"Here in Baja?" she asked.

"Yeah. My mom is Mexican. She's from Mulegé."

"Really?" Bridget asked, genuinely interested. That explained his looks. "Just a few miles south of here, right?"

"Right," he agreed. "What about you?"

"I'm from Washington, D.C. My dad is from Amsterdam."

"Wow. So you know the whole foreign-parent syndrome."

She laughed, pleased at how this was going. "I do."

"What about your mom?" And here, without warning, she'd come directly to a second test. This was one she usually saved for much further down the road if she could.

"My mom . . ." Is? Was? She was still indecisive about tense when it came to this. "My mom . . . was from Alabama. She died." Bridget had spent four years saying her mother "passed away," but then the term started to really annoy her. It didn't fit with what had happened.

He turned his head and looked at her straight on. "I'm so sad for you."

She felt the sweat dry up on her skin. It was a disarmingly honest thing to say. She looked away. At least he hadn't said, "I'm sorry." She suddenly felt exposed in her running bra.

With most guys she managed to forestall this issue indefinitely. She'd gone out with guys for months at a time and not had this conversation. It was strange that with Eric it had come up in the first two minutes. Carmen would take that as a sign of something, but then Carmen was always looking for signs. Bridget never did.

"You go to Columbia now?" she asked, leaving her discomfort on the path behind them.

"Yeah."

"Do you like it?"

"It's a strange school for an athlete," he said. "Sports aren't exactly a big emphasis there."

"Right."

"But it's got a great soccer program, and the academics are obviously good. That was a big deal to my mom."

"Makes sense," she said. His profile was awfully nice.

He was picking up the pace now. She took that as a challenge. She always enjoyed a challenge.

She glanced back to see that the group had thinned a lot. She kept with him stride for stride. She loved the feeling of strain in her muscles, the exhilaration that came with mounting exhaustion.

"How old are you?" he asked her point-blank.

She was hoping to finesse this issue. She knew she was among the youngest girls here. "Sixteen," she answered. She would be soon. It wasn't a crime to round up, was it? "What about you?"

"Nineteen," he answered.

That wasn't such a big difference. Particularly if she were sixteen.

"Are you thinking about colleges yet?" he asked.

"Maybe University of Virginia," she said. She actually had no idea. The truth was, the coach at UVA had already commented on Bridget to her high school coach. Bridget knew she didn't have to worry much about college, even if her grades weren't that spectacular.

"Great school," he said.

Now she was pushing the pace. She was feeling good, and the excitement of being this close to Eric was energizing her muscles. They circled back around to finish the run up the beach.

"You must be pretty serious about running," he said to her.

She laughed. "I haven't run in months." And with that, she accelerated to a near sprint. The rest of the group had fallen far behind. She was curious to see whether Eric would stick to his preset pace or abandon it to keep up with her.

She felt his elbow brush hers. She smiled. "Race ya."

They sprinted the half mile up the beach. There was so much adrenaline filling Bridget's veins, she could have flown the distance.

She collapsed on the sand. He collapsed too. "I think we set a record," he said.

She spread out her arms, happy. "I've always been goal oriented." Bridget rolled around in the sand until she was covered like a sugar doughnut. He watched her, laughing.

The rest of the group would catch up in a couple of minutes. She stood and kicked off her shoes and socks. She looked right at him when she pulled off her shorts, revealing her bikini bottoms; then she yanked the elastic out of her hair. Yellow clumps stuck to her sweaty shoulders and back.

He looked away.

"Let's swim," she said.

His face was serious now. He didn't move.

She didn't wait for him. She waded in several yards and then dove under. When she came up, she saw that he had stripped off his soaked T-shirt. She didn't pretend not to stare.

Eric dove in after her, just as she prayed he would. He swam past where she was and surfaced a few yards away.

Bridget raised her arms in the air for no reason. She jumped up and down in the water, unable to contain her energy. "This is the best place in the world."

He laughed again, his serious face gone.

She dove under the surface and plummeted to the sandy bottom. Slowly she passed his feet. Without thinking, she reached out her hand and touched his ankle with her finger, light as a triggerfish.

When life hands
you a lemon, say,
"oh yeah, I like
lemons. What else
ya got?"
—Henry Rollins

When Lena arrived in the kitchen the next morning for breakfast, only her grandfather was awake. *"Kalemera,"* she said.

He nodded and blinked in acknowledgment. She sat down across from him at the small kitchen table. He pointed the box of Rice Krispies at her. She happened to love Rice Krispies. *"Efcharisto,"* she thanked him, about reaching the limits of her Greek. Grandma had left out bowls and spoons. Bapi handed her the milk.

They chewed. She looked at him, and he looked into his bowl. Was he annoyed because she was there? Did he like to eat breakfast alone? Was he very disappointed that she couldn't speak Greek?

He poured himself another bowl of cereal. Bapi was kind of wiry, but he clearly had a good appetite. It was funny. As she looked at Bapi, she recognized some of her own features. The nose, for instance. Almost everybody else in the family had the famous Kaligaris nose—her father, her aunt, Effie. The big, prominent nose gave character to all who wore it. Of course, her mother had a different nose—a Patmos nose—but even that was sufficiently distinctive.

Lena's nose was small, delicate, characterless. She'd always wondered where she'd gotten it, but now she saw it right in the middle of Bapi's face. Did that mean that *she* had the true Kaligaris nose? Since she was small she'd secretly wished she had the big family nose. Now that she saw where she got hers, she liked it a little better.

She made herself stop looking at Bapi. She was no doubt making him uncomfortable. She should definitely say something. It was probably very awkward for her to sit here and not be saying anything.

"I'm going to make a painting this morning," she said. She gestured like she was painting.

He seemed to snap out of his cereal reverie. She knew that feeling so well. He raised his eyebrows and nodded. Whether he understood a word, she couldn't tell.

"I was thinking I'd walk down to Ammoudi. Are there stairs all the way down?"

Bapi considered and nodded. She could tell he wanted to get back to his contemplation of the cereal box. Was he tired of her? Was she annoying him?

"Okay, well, I'll see you later. Have a good day, Bapi. *Andio.*"

She walked upstairs and packed up her painting things with the oddest feeling that she was Effie and she'd just eaten breakfast with herself.

She put on the Pants with a wrinkly white linen shirt. She slung her backpack, containing her palette, her foldable easel, and her panels, over her shoulder.

Just as she reached the stairs, Kostos arrived at the front door, delivering a platter of freshly baked pastries from his grandmother. Grandma hugged him and kissed him and thanked him in such fast Greek that Lena couldn't make out a single word.

Grandma spotted Lena and got that look in her eye. Quickly she invited Kostos inside.

Lena wished Effie were awake. She made for the door.

"Lena, sit down. Have a pastry," Grandma ordered.

"I'm going painting. I need to get started before the sun gets too high and the shadows disappear," Lena claimed. It wasn't technically true, because she was starting a new painting today, which meant the shadows could be any which way.

Kostos migrated toward the front door himself. "I have to get to work, Valia. I'm late already."

Grandma happily settled for the idea that at

least the two would have to walk together outside. Grandma winked at Lena as she followed Kostos out the door. "He's a *nice* boy," she stage-whispered to Lena. It was Grandma's constant refrain.

"You love to paint," Kostos observed once out in the sunshine.

"I do," Lena said. "Especially here." She wasn't sure why she offered that last gratuitous bit.

"I know it's beautiful here," Kostos said thoughtfully, looking out over the glittering water. "But I can hardly see it. These are the only views I know."

Lena felt the desire for a real conversation coming on. She was interested in what he said. Then she thought of her grandmother, probably watching them through the window.

"Which way are you walking?" Lena asked. It was a slightly mean trick she was setting up.

Kostos looked at her sideways, clearly trying to gauge what the best answer would be. Honesty prevailed. "Downhill. To the forge."

Easy enough. "I'm heading uphill. I'm going to paint the interior today." She began drifting away from him, up the hill.

He was obviously unhappy. Did he discern that she'd set him up? Most boys weren't that sensitive to rejection.

"Okay," he said. "Have a good day."

"You too," she said breezily.

It was kind of a shame in a way, walking uphill, because she'd woken today with a real lust to paint the boathouse down in Ammoudi.

Tibba-dee,

You would hate this place. Wholesome, all-American people doing sports all day. High fives are common. I even witnessed a group hug. Sports clichés all day long.

Almost makes you happy to be at Wallman's, don't it?

Just kidding, Tib.

Of course, I love it. But every day I'm here, I'm glad my real life is not like this, full of people like me, 'cause then I wouldn't have you, would I?

Oh, I'm in love. Did I tell you that yet? His name is Eric. He's a coach and 100% off-limits. But you know how I get.

Love your BFF,
Bee

When Tibby got back to Wallman's, she discovered two things: first, that she had "performed a firable offense" by skipping out on so much of her shift (as Duncan had wasted no time in informing her). She could have a last chance, but she wouldn't be paid for the part of the day she did work. Tibby was beginning to think she would owe money to Wallman's at the end of this job.

The second discovery was the fainting girl's wallet lying next to her own wallet in her plastic, see-through bad-employee bag. Oh, shit.

She found the library card listing the girl's name: Bailey Graffman. Tibby walked outside to the pay phone. The white pages, thank goodness, listed one Graffman with two *f*s on a street near Wallman's.

Tibby got right back on her bike and rode the few blocks to the Graffmans'. A woman she guessed was Mrs. Graffman opened the door. "Hi. Uh, my name is Tibby and I, uh . . ."

"You're the one who found Bailey at Wallman's," the woman said, looking fairly appreciative.

"Right. Well, it turns out I took her wallet to find contact information and I, uh, forgot to give it back," Tibby explained. "There were only four dollars in it," she added defensively.

Mrs. Graffman looked at Tibby in confusion. "Um. Right. Of course." Then she smiled. "Bailey's resting upstairs. Why don't you give it to her? I'm sure she'll want to thank you personally.

"Upstairs and straight ahead," the woman instructed as Tibby trudged up the steps.

"Uh, hi," Tibby said awkwardly at the girl's

door. The room was decorated with ribbon wallpaper and puffy yellow curtains, but there were boy-band posters every few feet. "I'm, uh, Tibby. I—"

"You're the girl from Wallman's," Bailey said, sitting up.

"Yeah." Tibby walked close to the bed and offered the wallet.

"You ripped off my wallet?" Bailey demanded with narrowed eyes.

Tibby scowled. What an obnoxious little kid. "I didn't *rip off* your wallet. The hospital used it to contact your parents and I held on to it. You're welcome." She tossed it on the bed.

Bailey grabbed it and looked inside, counting the bills. "I think I had more than four dollars."

"I think you didn't."

"'Cause you took it."

Tibby shook her head in disbelief. "Are you joking? Do you seriously think I would steal your money and then come all the way over here to deliver your pathetic little wallet? What's there to return other than the money? Your horoscope? Avert a big emergency in case you forget your moon sign?"

Bailey looked surprised.

Tibby felt bad. Maybe she'd overdone it.

Bailey didn't back down, though. "And what

important stuff have you got in *your* wallet? A license to ride your bike? A *Wallman's* employee ID?" She said "Wallman's" with more scorn than even Tibby could muster.

Tibby blinked. "How old are you? Ten? Who taught you to be so vicious?"

Bailey's eyebrows descended angrily. "I'm twelve."

Now Tibby felt worse. She'd always hated people who assumed she was younger than she was just because she was small and skinny and flat-chested.

"How old are *you*?" Bailey wanted to know. She had an excited, combative look in her eye. "Thirteen?"

"Bailey! Time to take your medicine," Bailey's mom called up the stairs. "Do you want to send your friend down?"

Tibby looked around. Was she supposed to be the "friend"?

"Sure," Bailey called back. She looked amused. "Do you mind?"

Tibby shook her head. "Of course not. Considering how you accept favors." Tibby trudged back downstairs wondering what in the world she was doing there.

Mrs. Graffman handed her a tall glass of orange juice and a little paper cup full of pills. "Everything okay up there?" she asked.

"Uh, I guess," Tibby answered.

Mrs. Graffman searched Tibby's face for a moment. "Bailey likes to test people," she offered for no particular reason.

"Tibby likes to test people." It was creepy. How many times had she heard her own mother say those exact words?

"I'm sure it's because of her illness."

Tibby didn't think before she asked, "What illness?"

Mrs. Graffman looked surprised that Tibby didn't know. "She has leukemia." Mrs. Graffman sounded like she was trying to be matter-of-fact. Like she'd said the word a million times and it didn't scare her anymore. But Tibby could see that it did.

Tibby felt that falling feeling. Mrs. Graffman looked at her with too much intensity, as though Tibby could say something that mattered. "I'm sorry to hear that," she mumbled stiffly.

Tibby made herself go back up the stairs. There was something too sad about the searching look of a sick kid's mother.

She paused at Bailey's door, sloshing the orange juice a little, feeling horrible for the mean things she'd said. Granted, Bailey had started it, but Bailey had leukemia.

Bailey was sitting up in bed now, looking eager to get back to the battle.

Tibby plastered some approximation of a bland, friendly smile on her face. She handed Bailey her pills.

"So anyway, did you lie about your age at Wallman's to get the job? Isn't the minimum age fifteen?" Bailey asked.

Tibby cleared her throat, careful to keep her smile from sagging. "Yeah. And actually, I am fifteen."

Bailey was clearly annoyed. "You don't look fifteen."

The smile was strained. Tibby couldn't remember how a regular smile was supposed to feel. This one had probably degraded into a grimace. "I guess not," Tibby said quietly. She really wanted to leave.

Bailey's eyes suddenly filled with tears. Tibby looked away. "She told you, didn't she?" Bailey demanded.

"Told me what?" Tibby asked the blanket, hating herself for pretending not to know when she knew perfectly well. She hated when people did that.

"That I'm sick!" Bailey's tough face was holding up about as well as Tibby's friendly smile.

"No," Tibby murmured, hating her own cowardice.

"I didn't think you were a liar," Bailey shot back.

Tibby's eyes, searching for any destination other

than Bailey's face, landed on a piece of netted cloth stuck through with needle and a piece of red yarn lying on Bailey's bedspread. Neat stitches spelled YOU ARE MY. What? Sunshine? The thing struck Tibby as tragic and sort of pathetic.

"I'd better go," Tibby said in a near whisper.

"Fine. Get out of here," Bailey said.

"Okay. See you around," Tibby said robotically. She shuffled toward the door.

"Nice smock," Bailey practically spat at her back.

"Thanks," Tibby heard herself saying as she fled.

Dear Carmen,

Some summer I want all of us to come here together. That is the happiest thing I can imagine. The first day I walked about a million steps down the cliffs to a tiny fishing village called Ammoudi on the Caldera. Caldera means "cauldron." It's this body of water that filled in after a monster volcano exploded and sank most of the island. After I painted these pretty Greek boats, it got to be broiling hot, so I stripped down to my bathing suit and dove right into the clear, cold water.

I made a painting for you. It's the bell tower right here in Oia. My shy grandpa, who doesn't speak

English, came around and studied my painting for a long time. He nodded approvingly, which was pretty cute.

Effie and I rode mopeds to Fira, the biggest village on the island, and drank unbelievably strong coffee at an outdoor café. We were both strung out on caffeine. I got anxious and silent, and Effie flirted outrageously with the waiters and even random passersby (passerbys?).

There's this guy Kostos. He walks past our house about six times a day. He keeps trying to catch my eye and start a conversation, but I won't play. My grandmother's dearest hope is that we'll fall in love. What could be less romantic than that?

Other than that, nothing really big has happened. Nothing big enough for the Pants. They're still waiting here patiently.

I can't wait to get a letter from you. The mail is so slow here. I wish I had a computer. I hope you and Al are having the very best time.

Love you,
Lena

＊　　＊　　＊

What am I doing here? Carmen gazed around the noisy room. Not a single noise or face distinguished itself in her ears or eyes. It was just random South Carolina teenagerness.

Krista was chattering with her friends in the backyard. Paul was being important with his babe-like girlfriend and jock buddies. Carmen stood alone by the staircase, forgetting to care that she looked like an unforgivable loser.

She felt weirdly numb and invisible. It wasn't just that she missed her friends; she was starting to wonder if she needed them around to feel like she existed at all.

Lydia and her dad had tickets to a chamber-orchestra concert. (For the record, her dad hated classical music.) They thought that Carmen going to a "fun party" with Krista and Paul would make everything good. Even a sullen girl who'd spent the last four days pouting in the guest room couldn't resist a "fun party." Her father looked so depressingly hopeful at the idea, she'd just gone. What did it matter?

A short guy sideswiped her shoulder. "Sorry," he said, spilling half his plastic cup of beer on the carpet. He stopped and looked at her. "Hey," he said.

"Hey," Carmen mumbled back.

"Who are you?" he asked. He looked at her breasts as though he were asking them.

She crossed her arms. "I'm, uh, Krista and Paul Rodman's, uh . . . Their mom is my . . ."

His eyes were now wandering away from her. She didn't bother to finish her sentence. Who cared?

"See you later," she said, and walked away.

Suddenly she was standing next to Paul. This was pitiful. He nodded at her. He was holding a Coke. He was probably between beers. "Have you met Kelly?" he asked. Kelly had her arm snaked around Paul's waist. She was so attractive as to actually be ugly. Her cheekbones were too prominent, her eyes too far apart, and her skinny collarbones jutted out.

"Hi, Kelly," Carmen said wearily.

"And you are?" Kelly asked.

"I'm Carmen," Carmen said. She could tell Kelly was threatened that Paul knew a girl she didn't know. And considering that Paul said a total of about seven words per day, he most likely hadn't explained to Kelly that there was a girl living in his house. "I live with Paul," she said just to be devious.

Kelly's narrow eyebrows ascended to her hairline. Carmen then glided away. "I'm going to get a drink," she murmured, casting flirtatious eyes at Paul.

Poor Paul. This would take him a year's worth of words to explain.

I have seen the future and it's like the present, only longer.
—Dan Quisenberry

"Tibby, will you cut up Nicky's chicken?" Tibby's mom asked.

Usually Tibby would have complained, but tonight she just leaned over and did it. Nicky seized her knife. "Me wanna cut! Me wanna!"

Patiently Tibby unwound his fat, sticky fingers from the butter knife. "No knives for babies, Nicky," Tibby droned, sounding exactly like her mother.

Nicky expressed his feelings by picking up two big handfuls of his noodles and throwing them on the floor.

"Grab it!" her mother instructed.

Tibby did. There was always that moment at dinner when Nicky started throwing his food on the ground. The trick was to pick the moment to grab his plate.

Tibby gazed forlornly at the noodles lying on the synthetic washable blue carpet. It was so resistant to stains, Tibby suspected it was made of Saran Wrap. There used to be a straw rug that itched her feet. There used to be Mexican candlesticks and salt and pepper shakers Tibby herself had made from clay. Now there were ones from Pottery Barn. Tibby couldn't say exactly the day when her salt and pepper shakers disappeared, but she could date it generally. It happened not too long after her mom stopped being a sculptor and took a test to become a real estate agent.

"Eegurt! Me want eegurt!" Nicky demanded.

Tibby's mom sighed. She was feeding a bottle of milk to a very sleepy Katherine. "Tibby, would you mind getting him a yogurt?" she asked wearily.

"I'm still eating," Tibby complained. Particularly on the nights her dad worked late, her mom expected Tibby to step in and be her coparent. Like Tibby had decided to have these kids with her. It was irritating.

"Fine." Tibby's mom stood up and plunked Katherine in Tibby's lap. Katherine started crying. Tibby stuck the bottle back in her mouth.

When Tibby was little, her dad had worked as a journalist and a public defender and briefly as an organic farmer, and he was always home for dinner. But after her mom started spending her time in people's big, clean houses and seeing all the nice things they had, her dad started practicing law in a private firm, and now he was only home about half the nights. It seemed poor planning to Tibby to have these extra kids and then never be home anymore.

Her parents used to talk about simplicity all the time, but nowadays they seemed to spend all their time getting new stuff and not having very much time to play with it.

Nicky was digging both hands in his yogurt and then licking his fingers. Tibby's mother snatched the yogurt away, and Nicky started howling.

Tibby had thought about mentioning Bailey and her leukemia to her mom, but as usual, it was hard to see where any conversation would fit in.

She went up to her room and recharged the batteries for her camera. She gazed at her sleeping computer, the Power button pulsing under its masking tape like a slow heartbeat.

Usually her computer was flashing and whirring all evening as she IMed her friends. Tonight they were all far away. Somehow the masking tape looked like a gag over the computer's mouth.

"Hey, Mimi," she said. Mimi was sleeping. Tibby added some food to Mimi's dish and changed her water. Mimi stayed asleep.

Later, as Tibby began to doze off with her lights and clothes still on, her thoughts came unstuck in that way they did, and she thought of geriatric diapers and antiperspirant and sterile wipes and bacteria-free soap and extra-absorbent panty shields and Bailey lying in a mess on the floor.

"There's your boyfriend," Diana said, watching Eric as he strode onto the deck.

Bridget fixed her eyes on him. *Look up, you.*

He did. Then he looked away so fast it was almost gratifying. He noticed her, all right.

He took a seat on the other side of the deck. Bridget dug into her lasagna. She was starving. She loved institutional food served in big quantities. She was weird that way.

"He probably has a girlfriend in New York," a girl named Rosie said.

"We'll see about that," Bridget said provocatively.

Diana shoved her elbow. "Bridget, you're insane."

Emily was shaking her head. "Give it up. You'll get in huge trouble."

"Who's gonna tell?" Bridget asked.

Diana put on her Sigmund Freud expression. "Anyway, getting in trouble is kind of the point, isn't it?"

"Of course it's not the point," Bridget said snappishly. "Have you taken one *look* at the guy?"

She stood up and walked to the buffet table to get

another helping of lasagna. She took a circuitous route in order to pass Eric. She knew her friends would be watching.

She stopped right behind him. She waited for a pause in the conversation he was having with Marci, his assistant coach. She leaned over. The place was noisy, so it was perfectly understandable that she should lean close to his ear. A curtain of her hair fell forward as she leaned, brushing his shoulder. "What time is the scrimmage?" she asked.

He hardly dared turn his head. "Ten."

She was making him nervous. "Okay. Thanks." She stood back up straight. "We'll kill y'all."

Now he turned to look at her, surprised and almost angry. Immediately he saw from her face that she was teasing him. "We'll see about that." At least he was smiling.

She drifted to the serving table, allowing herself one quick glance at her friends' impressed faces. "Ha," she mouthed.

Dear Carmen,
    The cabin girls have upped my odds with Eric to 40/60. I'm being very flirtatious and very bad. You would laugh. What's a girl to do, stuck a thousand miles out here in the ocean?

We went sight-seeing in the closest town, Mulegé. That's where Eric's mom is from. We saw this big mission church and a prison called <u>carcel sin cerraduras</u>—prison without locks. They let the prisoners work on farms in the daytime and come back to their cells to sleep at night.

Hope you're having fun hanging with Al.

All love,
Bee

Lena had one more day with the Pants, and she had to make them count. So far, she'd been her usual lame self: solitary and routine-loving, carefully avoiding any path that might lead to spontaneous human interaction. She was, overall, a terrible first escort for the Traveling Pants.

Today, though, she'd have an adventure. She'd do something. She wouldn't let her friends down. Or the Pants. Or herself, come to think of it.

She walked up, up, over the crest of the cliff and onto the flat land at the top. It was much emptier up here. In the distance hills rose, probably signaling yet a higher cliff plunging into the sea. But here the land was gentle. Though it was arid, rocky cliff smoothed into wide green vineyards and meadows. The air felt hotter and the sun even stronger.

These are lucky pants, she thought a half mile or so later when she came upon an exquisite little arbor. It was a perfect grove of olive trees with glinting silver-green leaves. The olives were small and hard—still babies. At one end she discovered a small spring-fed pond. It was so private, so quiet, so lovely, it felt like her place—like she was the first person ever to set eyes on it. Like maybe it had never even existed before she got here with her magic pants. Immediately she set up her easel and began to paint.

By the time the sun had risen to the top of the sky, Lena was bathed head to toe in salty sweat. The sun beat down so hard it made her dizzy. Sweat dripped down from her thick, dark hair onto her neck and temples. She wished she'd brought a hat. She cast a longing glance at the pond. More than that, she wished she'd remembered to bring her bathing suit.

She looked around. There was no one as far as she could see. She couldn't make out a single house or farm. She felt a little creek of sweat flowing down her spine. She had to get into that pond.

Shy even with herself, Lena took off her clothes slowly. *I can't believe I'm doing this.* She stripped down to her bra and underwear, casting her clothing into a pile. She considered wearing her underclothes into the water, but that seemed embarrassingly prudish. She looked at the Pants. They challenged her to get naked fast.

"Ahhhhhhh," Lena said as she waded in. It was funny to hear her voice aloud. Her thoughts and perceptions usually existed so deep inside her, they rarely made it to her surface without a deliberate effort. Even when she saw something genuinely funny on television, she never laughed out loud when she was alone.

She ducked all the way under the water and then came up again. She floated languidly with just her face above the surface. The sun warmed her cheeks and eyelids. She splashed a little, loving the swish of water over every part of her body.

This is the most perfect moment of my life, she decided. She felt like an ancient Greek goddess alone under the sky.

She let her arms float out to her sides, tipped her head back, closed her eyes, and just levitated, every muscle loose and soft. She would stay this way until the sun set, until it rose again, until August, until maybe forever. . . .

Every muscle in her body snapped to attention at the sound of rustling grass. In a fraction of an instant she found her feet on the pebbly bottom of the pond and stood.

She drew in a sharp breath. Someone was there. She saw the shadow of a figure obscured behind a tree. Was it a man? An animal? Were there vicious, man-eating animals on Santorini?

Her peace was broken, smashed to bits. She felt her heart nearly bouncing out of her chest.

Fear told her to sink her body back underwater, but a bigger fear told her to run away. She pulled herself out of the pond. The figure emerged.

It was Kostos.

She was staring directly at Kostos, and, far worse, Kostos was staring directly at her. She was so stunned, she took a moment to react.

"K-Kostos!" she shouted, her voice a ragged shriek. "What are you—what—"

"I'm sorry," he said. He should have averted his eyes, but he didn't.

In three steps she'd reached her clothes. She snatched them and covered herself with the bundle. "Did you follow me?" she nearly screamed. "Have you been spying on me? How long were you here?"

"I'm sorry," he said again, and muttered something in Greek. He turned around and walked away.

Still soaking wet, she yanked on her clothes haphazardly. In a storm of anger she threw her paint supplies into her backpack, probably smearing her painting. She strode across the meadow and toward the cliff, too mad to link her thoughts.

He'd been following her! And if he . . . Her pants were inside out. How dare he stare at her like that! She was going to . . .

She realized, by the time she neared the house, that her shirt was off-kilter by two buttons, and between pond water and sweat it was stuck to her body almost obscenely.

She banged into the house and threw her backpack on the ground. Grandma sped out of the kitchen and gasped at the sight of her.

"Lena, lamb, vhat happened to you?"

Grandma's face was full of worry, and that made Lena want to cry. Her chin quivered the way it used to when she was five.

"Vhat? Tell me?" Grandma asked, gazing at Lena's inside-out pants and misbuttoned shirt with wide, confused eyes.

Lena sputtered for words. She tried to harness one or two of her spinning thoughts. "K-Kostos is *not* a nice boy!" she finally burst out, full of shaky fury. Then she stomped up to her room.

Sometimes you're
the windshield;
sometimes you're
the bug.

—Mark Knopfler

Carmen watched Krista struggling with her homework at the kitchen table. She was taking summer school geometry to lighten her load for junior year. Carmen had the impression Krista wasn't going to be joining Mensa or anything.

"You 'bout ready?" her dad called to her from his bedroom, where he was putting on his tennis clothes.

"Just about," Carmen called back. She'd been ready for the last twenty minutes.

Krista was doing a lot of erasing. She kept blowing red eraser bits over her scarred paper. She was like a third grader. Carmen felt a pang of sympathy for her and then beat it back. Carmen couldn't help glancing at the problems on Krista's paper. She'd taken geometry in ninth grade, math geek that she was, and it was possibly her favorite class ever. Krista was stuck on a proof. Carmen could tell by just squinting across the table exactly how to do it in a minimum of steps. It was weird, her longing to do that proof. Her fingers were practically tingling for the pencil.

She could hear Lydia blabbing on the phone in the den in her wedding voice. It was the caterer, Carmen guessed, because Lydia kept mentioning "miniature soufflés."

"All set?" her father asked, appearing at the kitchen door in his Williams T-shirt and his white tennis shorts.

Carmen got up, her heart lifting. This was the first thing she was doing with her father in the five long days she'd been there. She felt almost absurdly privileged to have him to herself.

She left the house with a sigh, sorry only to be leaving the geometry proof.

It wasn't until she was out the door that the thought occurred to her that if Krista weren't Krista, if she bore no relationship to Carmen's father, she would have asked Krista if she needed some help.

Dear Bee,

Skeletor came over again this afternoon. She's over here almost every hour that Paul is home. It's pretty sad that my only joy in life is tormenting that dumb girl. Today I put on a pair of boxers and a cut-off tank top and knocked on Paul's door and asked to borrow a nail clipper. It's clear that Paul completely hates me, though he never says anything, so it's hard to know. The idea that I would be attractive to Paul and a threat to his and Skeletor's happiness is preposterous. But she doesn't know that.

All love from your evil friend who has a tiny patch of heart left to miss her friends desperately,

Carmen

For some unaccountable reason, Bailey showed up at Wallman's the next day.

"What are you doing here?" Tibby asked, forgetting for a moment to be nice.

"I thought I'd give you another chance," Bailey said. She was wearing cargo pants almost identical to the ones Tibby had worn the day before. She had on a hoodie sweatshirt and a trace of black eyeliner. It was obvious she was trying to look older.

"What do you mean?" Tibby asked dumbly, once again disturbing herself with her quick willingness to lie.

Bailey rolled her eyes in annoyance. "Another chance not to be an asshole."

In spite of herself, Tibby's temper flared.

"Who's the asshole here?" she snapped.

Bailey smiled. "Hey, listen, is that smock your kind of one-size-fits-all item?"

"Yeah, wanna borrow it?" Tibby asked, enjoying the playfulness on Bailey's face.

"Nah. It's butt ugly," Bailey commented.

Tibby laughed. "It's two-ply. It's made of petroleum."

"Nice. You need some help with that?" Bailey asked.

Tibby was stacking boxes of tampons. "Are you looking to get a job at Wallman's?"

"No. I just feel bad I wrecked that deodorant display."

"Antiperspirant," Tibby noted.

"Right," Bailey said. She started stacking. "So, do you ever take the smock off? Or do you wear it around the clock?"

Tibby was annoyed. She couldn't take much more mocking about the smock. "Would you leave the smock alone?" she asked testily. She was tempted to bring up the needlepoint. Tibby's *mother* used to do needlepoint.

Bailey looked pleased. "For now." She pushed her hair out of her eyes. "Can I buy you some ice cream or something after your shift? You know, as thanks for not stealing *all* my money?"

Tibby didn't feel like hanging with a twelve-year-old. On the other hand, she didn't feel like she could say no. "Sure. I guess."

"Great," Bailey said. "What time?"

"I get off at four," Tibby said without enthusiasm.

"I'll come by," Bailey offered. She turned to go. "Are you just being nice to me because I have cancer?" she asked over her shoulder.

Tibby considered this for a moment. She could lie some more. Or not. She shrugged. "Yeah, I guess so."

Bailey nodded. "Okay."

Tibby quickly learned the ground rules with Bailey. It wasn't hard. There were only two of them: 1) Don't lie. 2) Don't ask her how she's feeling.

Other than that, the conversation over brownies with ice cream and chocolate sauce ranged far and wide. Tibby found herself talking with unusual interest and openness about the movie she was planning. Bailey acted like she was fascinated, and Tibby wasn't immune to a person thinking she was cool.

It made Tibby wonder about herself—if maybe she missed her friends even more than she had realized. Was she so lonely that she'd open up to any random annoying twelve-year-old?

Bailey seemed to have the same suspicion. "Do you have any friends?" she asked at one point.

"Yes," Tibby said defensively. But as she began to describe her three fabulous, beautiful, and amazing friends and the awesome places they were spending their summers, she realized it really sounded like she was making them up.

"Where are all of *your* friends?" Tibby finally asked, throwing the burden back to Bailey.

Bailey rattled on about Maddie, who lived in Minnesota now, and somebody else.

Tibby looked up at one point and saw Tucker Rowe standing at the counter. Her heart started beating faster. Was he the only other person in their class who was home this summer? She'd figured out by now that he worked at the ultrahip indie record store that shared a parking lot with Wallman's. It was a whole four stores over, past a Burger King, a pizza place, and Calling All Pets, so running into him wasn't a definite. But it was highly likely. It had happened once already.

Some people go out of their way to run into their crushes. Tibby did everything she could to avoid it. Mostly, she'd observed, Tucker parked in the back of the strip mall. So she always made it a point to park her bike in the front. And it seemed to work okay. Except for now, in this ice cream shop, which happened to be on the other side of Calling All Pets. Tibby silently berated herself for such bad planning.

Tucker was wearing a slight scowl and a squinty face that made him look like he'd only just gotten out of bed. He was probably hanging at the Nine Thirty Club all night while she was resting up for her next shift at Wallman's. She seriously hoped he would think that Bailey was her little sister and not her new best friend.

"Why are you holding your face like that?"

Tibby glared at Bailey. "What do you mean?"

"You know, with your cheeks all sucked in." Bailey did an exaggerated imitation.

Tibby felt her face warm. "I wasn't." When had Tibby started lying? She prided herself on being direct—with herself especially. But Bailey was far more ruthlessly direct than even Tibby, and it was causing Tibby to hide and shrink, just what Tibby accused other people of doing.

Bailey wasn't done yet. Her eagle eyes scanned the front of the store. "Do you like him?"

Tibby was about to pretend she didn't know who Bailey was talking about, but she stopped herself. "He's okay," Tibby agreed uncomfortably.

"You think?" Bailey looked unconvinced. "What do you like about him?"

"What do I like about him?" Tibby was annoyed. "Look at him."

Bailey stared at him baldly. Tibby felt embarrassed, even though she hated the whole giggly "Don't let him see you're looking at him" routine.

"I think he looks stupid," Bailey announced.

Tibby rolled her eyes. "You do, do you?"

"Does he really think those earrings are cool? And, I mean, look at his hair. How much gel went into that hair?"

Tibby had never considered that Tucker actually spent time trying to make himself look like he looked. It was true that the height of his hair looked less than accidental. Even so, she didn't feel like admitting that to Bailey.

"Um, no offense, Bailey, but you're twelve. You haven't even hit puberty yet. Please forgive me if I don't accept your expert testimony about guys," Tibby said snottily.

"No offense taken," Bailey said, obviously enjoying herself. "I'll tell you what. I'll find a worthwhile guy sometime, and you tell me if you don't agree."

"Fine," Tibby said, sure she wouldn't be spending enough time with Bailey to give her the chance to identify that worthwhile guy.

❄   ❄   ❄

"Uh-oh." Diana looked up from her book. "Bee has on her pirate face."

"I do not," Bridget protested, though she completely did.

Ollie was sitting cross-legged on her bed. A lot of girls in the cabin had already put on their nightshirts and stuff. "You want to raid the coaches' cabin?" Ollie asked.

Bridget raised her eyebrows in interest. "Actually, that sounds nice, but that's not what I was thinking."

"What were you thinking?" Diana asked like a know-it-all.

"Two words. Hotel Hacienda." It was the one bar in all of Mulegé, the place where she'd heard the coaches went at night.

"I don't think we're supposed to," Emily said.

"Why not?" Bridget demanded. "Ollie is seventeen. Sarah Snell is eighteen. Practically half the people here are going to college in the fall." She wasn't one of them, but she didn't feel the need to mention it. "This isn't Camp Kitchee where you turn off your flashlights at nine. I mean, come on. There's not even a drinking age in Mexico." She didn't actually know whether that was true or not.

"The first scrimmage is tomorrow," Rosie pointed out.

"So? Partying makes you play better," Bridget said blithely. There was a statement that belonged with "Drinking makes you drive better," or "Getting stoned makes you good at physics," but who cared? She was in one of her impulsive moods.

"How do we go?" Diana asked. She was practical, but she wasn't a coward.

Bridget considered. "We could either steal a van or take bikes. I think it's about half an hour on bikes if you ride fast." Bridget didn't want to volunteer the fact that she didn't have a driver's license yet.

"Let's take bikes," Ollie said.

Bridget felt that slightly reckless fizz in her veins she always got when she was doing something she shouldn't.

Diana, Ollie, and Rosie were in. The rest were out. They quickly changed their clothes. Bridget borrowed a skirt from Diana, who was almost as tall as she was. It was annoying that Bridget hadn't thought to bring clothes that didn't make her look like a boy.

Four of them flew along the Baja Highway, whizzing past snail-like RVs. Bridget kept bumping against Diana's back tire and making her scream. The placid bay was to their left and the hills were to their right, and the full moon sat on Bridget's shoulder.

They could hear the music throbbing from the hotel before it came into sight. "Wahooo!" Bridget yelled. They made a quick huddle at the door.

"Listen," Ollie said. "If Connie's there, we leave. I don't think anyone else will care. We went a couple times at the end of last year, and none of the coaches said anything."

Ollie elected herself the one to check. She ducked in and came right back out. "It's packed, but I didn't see her. If she shows, we leave." She looked at Bridget dubiously. "Okay?"

"Okay," Bridget agreed.

"Whether or not Eric is there."

"I said okay."

Bridget hadn't been to many clubs, but each time was the same. All eyes, at least all male eyes, followed her hair. Maybe it was the combination of bar light and alcohol that made it glow extra bright.

They made for the dance floor. Bridget was indifferent to drinking, but she loved to dance. She grabbed Diana's hand and pulled her onto the crowded dance floor. Dancing was like soccer or miniature golf or gin rummy. It was just one of those things she was good at.

The salsa music pounded through her body. There were shouts and stares and catcalls that she suspected were aimed at her—or her hair, anyway. She looked for Eric.

At first she didn't see him, so she gave her whole self to the music. A little while later she spotted him with other coaches at a table away from the dancing. The table was covered with big, salty margarita glasses, mostly empty.

He was watching her. He didn't see her see him seeing her yet, and she didn't want him to. She made it a point never to be coy, but she wanted him to be able to watch her if he wanted to.

He looked mellow from sun and running and probably tequila. He had a sexy way of tipping his head to the side when he looked at people.

Men kept bobbing around her, but she stuck with Diana, her preferred partner. A few minutes later, Ollie joined them, a beer in one hand.

Ollie spotted the coaches' table and waved to them. Marci waved back. Eric and another coach, Robbie, gave them looks that said, *We'll just pretend we're not seeing this.*

But another round of margaritas later, the coaches were out on the dance floor too. It was heady and good. Bridget felt a dancing high coming on that rivaled her running high. She couldn't resist him anymore.

She turned to Eric and danced close. She touched his hand momentarily. She watched his hips. He was both easy and skilled. She let her eyes linger on his. For once he didn't look away.

She put her hands at the bottom of his back, matching her hips to his. He was so close she could smell his neck. He put his lips to her ear. It sent an avalanche of chills to her feet.

Gently he gathered her hands and gave them back. In her ear he whispered, "We can't do this."

Lena threw herself onto her bed, nearly exploding with self-concern. Then she heard whispers and then shouting downstairs. Was her silent grandfather shouting? She leaped to her feet and pulled off her wet shirt, replacing it with a dry one. Then she yanked off the Pants and put them on the right way, her fingers shaking. What was going on here?

When Lena arrived at the bottom of the stairs, she saw that Bapi's face was practically purple, and he was striding toward the front door. Grandma hovered around him, reasoning with him in a nervous tangle of Greek. Her words were not appearing to make much difference. Bapi stormed out the door and turned downhill.

Suddenly Lena was getting a bad feeling about this. She skittered behind them. She knew before Bapi reached the Dounas residence that he would be stopping there. He knocked violently on the door.

Kostos's grandfather opened the door. The man looked fully astounded at the expression on Bapi's face. Bapi Kaligaris started yelling. Lena heard him bellow the name Kostos a few times, but otherwise she understood only anger. Grandma fluttered around timidly.

Bapi Dounas's face transformed slowly from confusion to indignation. He started yelling back.

"Oh, God," Lena whimpered to herself.

Suddenly Bapi was forcing himself into the Dounas house. Grandma was trying to hold him back, and Bapi Dounas was planting himself in the way. *"Pou einai Kostos?"* Bapi thundered.

Lena was pretty sure that meant "Where is

Kostos?" Right then, Kostos appeared behind his grandfather, looking bewildered and upset. He obviously wanted to comfort Lena's grandfather, but his own grandfather wouldn't let him by.

Lena watched in acute horror as her *bapi* put his wiry arms out and tried to shove the other old man out of the way. Bapi Dounas's eyes bulged, and he shoved back. Suddenly Bapi Kaligaris cocked his arm and punched Bapi Dounas in the nose.

Lena gasped. Grandma screamed.

The old men each got in another punch before Kostos overpowered them both. He held them apart, his face gray with agitation. "*Stamatiste!*" he bellowed. "Stop!"

Dear Daddy,
Can you send more clothes? My tank tops and the sundresses in my third drawer down? Also, my black bathing suit—the two-piece? Oh, and skirts from the fourth drawer—the short pink one and the turquoise one?

I'm still loving it here. We have our first big scrimmage today, and I'm starting at forward. I'll call you again on Saturday. Say hi to Perry.

Love,
Bee

I f you feel like
you're under control,
you're just not going
fast enough.
—Mario Andretti

"Are you excited about your wedding?" Carmen asked her father as they drove, hoping her voice didn't sound sour.

"Oh, yeah," he said. "Can't wait." He looked at her affectionately. "And I can't tell you what it means to me that you'll be here, bun."

Carmen felt guilty. Why was she being this way? Why couldn't she stop, and be nice?

"I hope you like miniature soufflés," she said, for no reason.

Her dad nodded. "Lydia's taking care of all that."

"I notice she spends a lot of time on it," Carmen said evenly, both wanting and not wanting her father to understand her implied criticism.

"It means a lot to her. She wants every detail exactly right."

Fleetingly Carmen considered the nasty question of who was paying for all this.

"She didn't have a real wedding the first time," her father continued.

Carmen's brain leaped around to various possible scandals. A shotgun affair? An elopement? "Why not?"

"She was planning an elaborate wedding with her mother, but her mother died suddenly six weeks before the wedding. It absolutely broke her heart. Ultimately her wedding involved two witnesses and a justice of the peace."

Carmen felt sad and deflated. "That's awful," she murmured.

"Now is her chance, and I really want her to enjoy it."

"Yeah," Carmen mumbled. She considered this awhile. "What happened to her old husband?"

"They split up four or five years ago. He has a serious drinking problem. He's been in and out of treatment."

Carmen sighed again. This was sad. She didn't want to feel sorry for Lydia. That made it hard to dislike her. But she thought of Lydia with her dead mom and her drunk husband, and silent Paul with his messed-up dad. In that context, his silence seemed more like stoicism. And Krista, so obviously in awe of Carmen's solid, kind, functional dad . . . How grateful they must all feel for their new life with Al.

Carmen promised herself she would smile at

Lydia when they got home and ask at least two friendly questions about the wedding.

"Hey, do you mind if we make a stop before tennis? Paul is playing in this summer soccer league, and today is a big match. I promised I'd look in for a few minutes."

"Fine," Carmen grumbled, and she went right back to being mad.

Bridget went swimming by herself at dawn. When she got excited, she couldn't sleep. She swam far, far out in the hopes of seeing a dolphin, but there wasn't one today. On her way back to shore, she swam around the headlands that separated their beach from the main part of Coyote Bay. RVs dotted the sand. Ick.

She swam back to her beach and lay down on the sand. She fell asleep for another hour or so. Then she heard the breakfast rush. She raced back to the cabin to put on her clothes. She was starving as usual.

She carried her three boxes of Froot Loops, two cartons of milk, and her banana across the deck and sat next to Diana.

"Do you sleep?" Diana asked. "Where were you this morning?"

"Swimming," Bridget answered.

"Alone?"

"Sadly, yes."

She searched the tables for Eric. He wasn't there. Was he hungover from last night? Or just slaving over his playbook? The memory of dancing with him last night brought color to her cheeks. "We can't do this," he'd said. He hadn't said, "You can't do this."

"Let's go warm up," she said to Diana.

The first scrimmage started at nine. Team one, El Burro, was already beating team two, the Gray Whales, by two goals. Team three, recently dubbed Los Tacos, and team four, Los Cocos, had the other field for practice.

Bridget sat on the sidelines, watching Eric discuss strategy with Marci and a couple of his players.

She laced up her cleats. Some famous old actor, she couldn't think of which one, had said he began his character with his shoes. Bridget was her favorite self with her cleats on, whether she was clicking through locker rooms with her extra three quarters of an inch of height or tearing through soft grass on the field. Her cleats were beat up and muddy, molded perfectly to her feet. They made her walk like a jock, but she liked that too.

She looked at Eric till he glanced back. She smiled; he didn't. *You guys are toast*, she vowed to whomever besides her happened to be listening to her thoughts.

Her team's coach, Molly Brevin, called them all over.

Bridget put on her shin guards and pulled her hair back in an elastic. Ollie and Emily slapped her hands as she joined the group. It was their first time playing as a team.

Molly read out the starting positions, even though they all knew them. Bridget jumped up and down to keep her blood flowing.

"Yo, Tacos. Listen up. All I care about is passing," Molly proclaimed. "I mean it. I don't care what else you do in this scrimmage. You hog the ball, and you come out." Why did she look at Bridget when she said that?

The teams assembled on the field. Bridget passed by Diana and gave her a quick squeeze around her waist. Diana jumped in surprise. "You are so de-ad," Bridget teased like a five-year-old. She got in her position at center field and waited for the long whistle.

Bridget needed a single focus. She had too much energy, she knew, and a fair amount of raw, undisciplined talent. At almost every point in her life, she needed one simple, unified goal to keep her going forward fast. Otherwise there was the possibility of going backward, where she did not want to go.

Today her focus was Eric. It was showing him what she could do. He was the unifying idea that kept every one of her cells in line.

Her energy exploded as soon as the ball got

moving. She immediately stole the ball from Dori Raines and took it down the field. She positioned herself for an open shot on goal, gathered two of three defenders, then passed it to the open forward, Alex Cohen. Alex got bottled up and passed it back to Bridget.

When Bridget's focus was good, time slowed for her. She had time to make choices. She had time to size up the position and trajectory of the goalie. She drew back her leg and tucked her foot under the ball to give it a few feet of lift. It sailed right past the goalie's head. Her teammates engulfed her. Through the gaps between bodies and limbs, she saw Eric. He was talking to his subs on the sideline. She wanted him to notice her so much.

She'd keep stomping them till he did. She stole ball after ball. She felt a strange elasticity, the capability to be both infinitely good and infinitely mediocre, depending on her mood. Today she raised the ceiling on good. She crashed through it. She made other legitimately fine, consistent players look like they didn't belong on the field.

"Pass, Vreeland!" Molly bellowed at her. At a higher level of play, Bridget wouldn't be taking crap like this. When your player is in the zone, you let her play. You give her the ball.

Bridget passed. The ball came back quickly. Her teammates acknowledged her power right now, even if her coach wouldn't. She scored again. Was it the third or the fourth?

Molly looked mad. She signaled to the ref, who blew her whistle. "Sub!" Molly shouted. "Come on out, Vreeland."

Bridget was mad right back. She strode to the sidelines and sat down on the grass, her chin in her hands. She wasn't even winded yet.

Molly came over. "Bridget, this is a *scrimmage*. Everybody needs to play. The point is for me to see what we have here. You're a superhero. I see that, and so does everybody else, all right? Save it for the championship."

Bridget put her head down. She suddenly felt all that intensity crashing in on her. She felt like crying.

She now knew she should have toned it down. Why was it so hard for her to make herself stop?

Dear Tibby,

Grilled shrimp canapés, salmon gravlax (what the hell is that?), crisped spinach, and roast pork loin. The flower arrangements involve tuberose (huh?) and magnolia blossoms (her favorite!). I could go on for another forty-five pages, Tib, but I'll spare you. It is ALL ANYBODY TALKS ABOUT in this place—of those people who actually talk, I mean. I'm going out of my mind. What has my dad gotten into?

Love and bitterness,
Carmen Lucille

"Which one is yours?" Carmen overheard a man ask her dad.

She was standing glumly a few yards away on the sidelines. Paul was the star of the team. In the eight minutes they had been there, he'd already scored two goals. Her dad was cheering like crazy. Down near the goal was Skeletor, made up nicer than a flight attendant. Every few seconds she took breaks from her hysterical enthusiasm to give Carmen a mean look.

"Which one is mine?" her dad repeated in confusion.

"Which is your kid?" the man clarified.

Her dad hesitated, but not for long enough. "Paul Rodman. He's playing forward." Her dad pointed.

Carmen felt a little chill zap along her spine and up into her scalp.

"He's an unbelievable player," the man said. He turned to look at her father. "He's built a lot like you," he said, then moved along the sideline to follow the progress of the ball.

How can he be built like you? He's not your kid!
Carmen felt like screaming at the top of her lungs.
I'm your kid!

Her dad came over and put his arm around her
shoulders. It didn't feel as good as it had five days ago.

Now you've got the son you always wanted,
Carmen thought bitterly. She knew he'd wanted
that. How could he not? He had a crabby ex-wife,
a sullen daughter, four crazy sisters. Here was a
big, silent, uncomplicated boy built just like him.

Carmen felt sick to her stomach. Paul scored
another goal. She hated him for it.

She was awful at soccer. When she was six
she'd played in a kiddie league. She raced up and
down the field and never touched the ball once.
Her dad went to those games too.

"It's exciting, isn't it?" her father asked now.
"Do you mind if we stay the rest of the half?"

"Who, me? Mind?" Her tartness made no
apparent impact.

"Great. They've got plenty of courts at the
club. We shouldn't have any problem."

Suddenly Skeletor appeared. She smiled sweetly
at Carmen's dad. "Hi, Mr. Lowell, how are you?"
she tweeted.

"Fine, thanks, Kelly. Do you know my daughter, Carmen?" he asked.

Kelly worked to keep the disgust off her face.

"We go way back. Hi, Kelly," Carmen said.

"Hi," Skeletor said stiffly. She turned to Al. "Isn't Paul just doing fantastic? You must be *so proud* of him."

Carmen raised an eyebrow at her. Was Skeletor more intelligent than Carmen had imagined?

"Well, yes, of course," her father mumbled.

Neither Carmen nor her father picked up the thread of conversation. Skeletor had a low threshold for social awkwardness. "I'll see y'all later," she said to Al, heading back up the sideline. "Go, Paul!" she shrieked as Paul did something heroic.

Suddenly Carmen recognized the pale figure of Lydia practically running toward them from the parking lot.

As soon as Al saw her, he let go of Carmen's shoulders and hurried over to his wife-to-be. "What is it?"

"The Plantation. They called to say they overbooked. One of the weddings has to bow out. They said we were the second booking," Lydia explained breathlessly. Carmen could see the tears quivering between her eyelids.

"Darling," Al said, holding her protectively. "That's terrible. What can we do?" He drew her aside to talk in private. Her dad always had a natural instinct for privacy, even if what stood between him and privacy was just his daughter.

A minute later, her dad came back. "Carmen, I need to go over to the Plantation with Lydia. We'll play tomorrow, okay?"

It wasn't a kind of okay that required an okay back. He had already moved on to the next concern. "I'll leave my car keys with you, and Paul can drive you back home." He kissed her forehead. "Sorry, bun, we'll have our tennis game. Don't worry."

Carmen could have acted like a big girl, but instead she lay on the grass, right on the sideline. It was a lucky thing she'd turned invisible in South Carolina, because otherwise this might have been tacky behavior.

If she were real and not invisible, if she could get a look at herself through the eyes of her friends or her mother, she might have been able to examine her feelings. Alone, she felt floaty and transparent.

The sun shone nicely on her face. Eventually she heard the long whistle that signaled the end of the game. A shadow came over her. With her hand she blocked out enough sun to see that it was Paul. He looked at her for a minute. If he found her freakish, he didn't let on.

"Do you want to play tennis?" he asked.

It was their longest communication so far. She said yes.

She went on to cream him 6–0, 6–0.

The problem is not the problem. The problem is your attitude about the problem. Got that?
—Coach Brevin

Hours after the fight, Lena sat between the two surly old men in a clinic in Fira. Her grandmother had gone for coffee and snacks, but Lena suspected she could no longer tolerate the scowling and moaning. Clearly disturbed, Kostos had quickly returned to the forge. He didn't even look at Lena.

Bapi needed four stitches along his cheekbone, and though Bapi Dounas complained bitterly of a broken nose—it *had* bled a lot—he didn't actually have one. As Lena waited under the fluorescent lights without even the comfort of a *People* magazine, she noticed a speck of blood drying on the Pants. "I'm sorry," she quietly told them. She went to the bathroom and tried to dab at the speck with some wet toilet paper. For a moment she felt guilty, remembering the washing rule, but who wanted the blood of a cranky old Greek man on their magic pants for the rest of eternity?

She caught a glimpse of herself in the mirror. Her hair had dried funny from the pond water. It was slightly puffy, rather than smooth and straight. She had the sensation of being tipsy. She put her face right up to the mirror. *Is that really me?*

Returning to the waiting area, she saw how silly the grandfathers looked. Their plastic chairs were side by side, but in their efforts to spurn each other they were sitting almost back to back. Lena knew how ridiculous, how absurd—how comical, even— this whole thing was. But though it seemed funny, it didn't actually *feel* funny to her. It just felt bad. She felt ashamed. Obviously her grandmother believed that Kostos had physically attacked Lena, and she had told Bapi so. Now they both believed that their beloved Kostos was some kind of evil rapist.

Lena could see now how profoundly she had overreacted. She should have told Grandma the truth and not let her jump to dramatic conclusions.

So Kostos had spied on her. He'd seen her naked. It was a bad and stupid and juvenile thing to do. Even so, she'd felt relieved to see his big sturdy self intervening in the fight and calming the two men down before they killed each other.

Kostos had spied on her, and she was annoyed at him for that. But he hadn't done the things her grandparents believed he'd done.

Now what? When everything calmed down

and they'd all had a chance to rest, she would apologize to her grandparents and explain exactly what had happened.

And then she would explain it to Kostos.

And eventually everything would be fine.

Lena,

I played too hard at the scrimmage today. I need to chill. What do you say to me? Calm your body, Bee. I'm trying, but my legs have got the jumpies.

I'll go for a run. With Eric. I WANT him. Did I mention that? I know you are above your hormones, but some of us can't help ourselves.

Love,
Bee FF

"Hi, my name is Bailey Graffman. I'm a friend of Tibby's. Is she home?"

Tibby listened in astonishment at the top of the stairs as Bailey stood at the front door introducing herself to Loretta over the screams of a cranky Katherine. Had she saddled herself with a twelve-year-old stalker?

Tibby carefully put Mimi back in her box and prayed Loretta would somehow not know she was home. No luck. Sure enough, seconds later, Tibby heard Bailey hopping up the stairs.

"Hi," Bailey said, waving from the door of her room.

"Bailey, what are you doing here?"

Bailey made herself comfortable on Tibby's unmade bed. "I can't stop thinking about your movie. It sounds so cool. I want to help you."

"You can't. I haven't even started yet," Tibby protested.

"So you definitely need help," Bailey reasoned. "I'll be your cameraman. Or your sound man. Or your gaffer. Or your best boy."

"You don't look like a man or a boy," Tibby pointed out.

"Or I could just be your general assistant. You know, P.A. Carry your junk and stuff."

Bailey looked so genuinely excited, it was hard to turn her down.

"Thanks, but I really don't need any help," Tibby said.

Bailey was on her feet and examining Mimi. "Who's this?" she asked.

"It's Mimi. I've had her since I was seven," Tibby explained dully. She tended to act like she didn't care deeply about Mimi when she was around her friends.

"She's sweet," Bailey said. She made twitching-nose faces at Mimi. "Could I hold her?"

Since she was about eight, not a single person, except for Nicky, had ever expressed interest in holding Mimi. Maybe that was the fringe benefit of being friends with a little kid. "Sure."

Carefully, confidently, Bailey scooped her out of her box. Mimi didn't seem to mind. She settled her fat body into Bailey's chest. "Ooh. She's warm. I don't have any pets."

"She doesn't do much," Tibby said, feeling a bit disloyal to Mimi. "She's pretty old. She sleeps a lot."

"Is she bored in there, do you think?" Bailey asked.

Tibby had never really considered that. She shrugged. "I don't know. I think she's pretty happy with it. I don't think she longs for the wild or anything."

Bailey settled into a chair with Mimi. "Have you decided who's going to be your first interview?" she asked.

Tibby was about to say no. She stopped herself. "Probably Duncan, this freak at Wallman's," she answered.

"How's he a freak?" Bailey asked.

"God, he's just . . . he just speaks this other language. Assistant General Manager language. He thinks he's so important. It's fairly hilarious."

"Oh." Bailey scratched Mimi's stomach.

"Then there's this lady with unbelievable fingernails," Tibby continued. "And I think Brianna deserves a little airtime with her antigravitational hairdo. And there's this girl who works at the

Pavillion I'd love to interview. She can recite whole scenes from movies, but only really dumb ones."

Bailey fidgeted in her chair. "I always wanted to make a documentary," she said wistfully.

Tibby had a feeling she was about to play the leukemia card. "Why don't you make one?"

"I don't have a camera. I don't know how. I really wish you'd let me help you."

Tibby sighed. "You're trying to make me feel guilty because you have leukemia, aren't you?"

Bailey snorted. "Yeah. Pretty much." She held Mimi close. "Hey, was that your little sister down there?"

Tibby nodded.

"Big age difference, huh?"

"Fourteen years," Tibby said. "I also have a two-year-old brother. He's taking a nap."

"Wow. Did one of your parents remarry?" Bailey asked.

"No. Same parents. They got married to a new lifestyle."

Bailey looked interested. "How do you mean?"

"Oh, I don't know." Tibby sank down on her bed. "When my parents first had me, we lived in a tiny apartment over a diner on Wisconsin Avenue, and my dad wrote for a socialist newspaper while he was getting his law degree. Then, after he got burned out as a public defender, we lived in a trailer on two acres out past Rockville, and my dad learned organic farming while my mom made sculptures of feet. One whole spring we lived in a tent in Portugal." Tibby looked around. "Now we live like this."

"Were they very young when they had you?" Bailey asked.

"Nineteen."

"You were kind of like their experiment," Bailey said, putting the sleeping Mimi on her lap.

Tibby looked at her. She'd never thought those precise words, but they captured a feeling. "I guess so," she said with more openness than she'd intended.

"Then they got to be grown-ups and they wanted kids for real," Bailey speculated.

Tibby was both amazed and discomfited by the way this conversation was going. What Bailey said was exactly true. When all her parents' friends had started having kids, her parents had seemed to want another chance to do it right. With baby monitors and matching bumpers and little musical mobiles. Not like it was for Tibby, a little tangly-headed accessory kid getting pulled along for the adventure.

Bailey looked at her with large, sympathetic eyes. Tibby felt sad. She wasn't sure how she'd ended up talking about this stuff. She wanted to be by herself. "I've got to, uh, leave in a while. You'd better go," Tibby said.

For once Bailey wasn't pushy. She got up to go. "Put Mimi back, okay?"

❃   ❃   ❃

Tibby,

I am such a mess. Kostos caught me skinny-dipping, and I totally freaked. You know how I get about privacy. So I throw on my clothes all wrong (I actually managed to put the Pants on inside out—how's that for magical?) and go running home in a fit. My grandmother sees me and assumes something way worse than actually happened.

So then, oh, God, this is painful to recount, she tells my grandfather (in Greek obviously) what she thinks happened, and I am not kidding you, Bapi goes over to beat Kostos up. Kostos's grandfather won't let him in the house, so the two grandfathers get in a fist-fight. It sounds funny, I know, but it was horrible.

Now my grandparents are at war with their best friends, and Kostos totally hates me, and nobody but us knows what happened.

I have to just tell the truth, right?

This was my first big Traveling Pants episode. I'm not sure the Pants have the effect we were hoping for. Oh, and I got a little blood on them—which may further inhibit their magic (did my best to wash it out, though). I'm now sending them to you by Santorini's fastest mail (it could take a while). I know you'll do better with them than I did.

I wish you were here, Tib. No, scratch that. I wish we were together anywhere but here.

Love,
Lena

Carmen's dad and Lydia were still at a party. Her dad, who'd basically never had friends, was suddenly a social butterfly. Lydia's friends were all his friends, just like that. He stepped into a life readymade. House, kids, friends. What was strange was how little of an old life he'd had to bring with him.

Paul was out with Skeletor, and Krista was doing a home spa with two friends in her room. Krista had politely invited Carmen to join in, but the thought just depressed her. It made her miss her friends.

She was sick of the guest room. Every piece of furniture was draped with clothes; the rest were on the floor. She was a hypocrite, she knew. She made messes but couldn't tolerate them.

In the kitchen she saw that Krista had left her geometry homework on the table. Carmen eyed it lustfully. Krista had left off in the middle of the second proof, and there were eight more to do.

The house was silent. She grabbed the papers. She studied them and grabbed the pencil too. She began working. Geometric proofs were pure joy. You started out with both the problem and the solution.

Her focus was so complete she didn't realize Paul had come home until he was standing in the kitchen watching her. Thank goodness he was without Skeletor. He looked puzzled.

Warm blood rushed to her face. What reason could she possibly give for doing Krista's homework?

He lingered for another moment. "Night," he said.

"Paul, did you do my math homework?" Krista demanded the next morning at breakfast. Her tone fell somewhere between sulky and grateful.

It was Sunday, and Al had made pancakes for everyone. Now he cooked too! Lydia had even set the table with her special floral china. What a treat.

Paul didn't answer right away.

"Did you think I was too dumb to do it myself?" Krista demanded.

Probably, Carmen was tempted to say.

"I didn't," Paul answered with his usual economy.

Krista sat up straight in her chair. "Do the work or think I was dumb?"

"Either," he said.

"So who did?" Krista demanded.

Carmen waited for Paul's eyes to land on her. They didn't. He didn't say anything, just shrugged.

If Paul wasn't going to bust her, should she implicate herself? Carmen wondered.

"I better go," Paul said. "Thanks for the pancakes, Albert."

He exited the kitchen and scooped up a duffel bag sitting by the front door before leaving the house.

"Where's he going?" Carmen asked, though it was no business of hers.

Lydia and Krista exchanged a glance. Lydia

opened her mouth, then closed it again. "He's going to . . . see . . . a friend," she finally said.

"Oh." Carmen wasn't sure why this was such a difficult question.

"So guess what?" Lydia changed the subject chattily. "We've come up with a backup plan for the reception."

She was talking to Carmen. Carmen realized that was because she was the only one who didn't know about it already.

"Oh," Carmen said again. She knew she was supposed to ask what it was.

"It's going to be in our own backyard. We've rented a giant tent! Doesn't that sound like fun?"

"Yes, fun." Carmen took the last sip of her orange juice.

"I was so upset yesterday, you know," Lydia went on, "but I wanted to be brave. And Albert had this fantastic idea about having it here at home. I'm just thrilled with our solution."

"Sounds . . . thrilling," Carmen said. She would have felt guilty for being sarcastic, except no one else seemed to hear it.

"Listen, kid," her dad said, sliding his chair back from the table. "We'd better get going to the club."

Carmen shot to her feet. "Let's go." At last, their promised tennis game. She followed him out of the house and hopped into his new beige family car.

"Bun," he began once they'd pulled away from the house. "What I told you about Lydia's former husband. It's something I'd like you to keep to yourself. Lydia is very sensitive about it."

Carmen nodded.

"The reason I bring it up is because Paul is driving down to visit his father today. His dad's at a treatment center in Atlanta. Paul drives down once a month and usually stays over," her dad explained.

For some reason, that made Carmen feel like she might cry.

"What about Krista?" she asked.

"Krista prefers not to stay in contact with her dad. It upsets her too much."

She's ashamed of him, Carmen thought. Just like Lydia was obviously ashamed of him. Get a newer, better model and forget about the old one.

"You can't just abandon your family," Carmen murmured. Then she turned her face to the window, and for the first time in days she really did cry.

"I set up the first interview for our movie," Bailey claimed excitedly.

Tibby huffed loudly into the phone. "*Our* movie?"

"Sorry. Your movie. That I'm helping with."

"Who said you're helping?" Tibby asked.

"Please? Please?" Bailey begged.

"Come on, Bailey. Don't you have anything

better to do?" In the silence that followed, Tibby's words seemed to echo across the phone line. Maybe that was not a question you asked a girl with a serious illness.

"I scheduled the interview for four-thirty, after you get off work," Bailey persisted. "I can drop by your house and pick up the stuff if you want."

"Who are we supposedly interviewing?" Tibby asked warily.

"That kid who plays arcade games in the Seven-Eleven across from Wallman's? He has the ten high scores on the hardest machine."

Tibby snorted. "He sounds appropriately lame."

"So I'll see you later?" Bailey asked.

"I'm not sure what my plans are," Tibby said coolly, not convincing either of them that she had any other life right now.

Of course Bailey showed up the minute Tibby's shift ended.

"How ya doin'?" Bailey asked, like they were best friends.

Tibby felt the hours under the fluorescent lights searing her brain. "Dying slowly," she said. Instantly she regretted her words.

"So come on," Bailey said, holding up the camera. "There's no time to lose."

If you don't find it in the index, look very carefully throughout the entire catalog.

—Sears Roebuck catalog

Upon her first introduction to Brian McBrian, Tibby knew they'd come to the right place for a scorn fest. He was a caricature of a caricature of a loser. He was both skinny and doughy at the same time, his skin as white-blue as skim milk. He had unibrow syndrome, greasy hair the color of dog doo, mossy braces, and a spitty way of talking. Tibby had to hand it to Bailey.

He cranked on *Dragon Master* while they set up. Tibby watched Bailey with grudging admiration as she attached the external microphone to a makeshift boom. With all the ambient noise inside and outside the store, there was no way to get a reasonable interview without a directed microphone. Had Bailey really never done this before?

Tibby started by setting the scene. She moved from an extreme close-up of an unnaturally pink Hostess Snowball, to a tabloid rack trumpeting

Vanna White's alien baby, to a counter display of Slim Jims. She finished her continuous shot on the guy working behind the counter. He immediately slapped his hands over his face, as though Tibby were an investigative journalist from *60 Minutes*. "No camera! No camera!" he barked.

Tibby caught a shot of Bailey's laughing face in the camera as she moved to the front of the store. She got a shot of Brian from behind, his jumping angel bones as he wrestled the dragons; then she cut the camera to set up the interview. "Ready?" she asked.

He turned around. Bailey positioned the microphone. "Rolling," she warned him.

He didn't primp or stiffen or put his head at a weird angle the way many people did before a camera. He just looked at her dead-on.

"So, Brian, we hear you're quite a regular here at Seven-Eleven." Tibby assumed that truly dorky people were deaf to sarcasm.

He nodded.

"What kind of hours do you keep?"

"Uh, just pretty much one till eleven."

"Does the store actually close at eleven?" Tibby asked, her mouth crinkling up into a grin.

"No, that's my curfew," he explained.

"And during the school year?"

"During the school year I get here by three oh five."

"I see. No after-school activities or anything?"

Brian seemed to gather the implication of her question. He gestured out the front glass of the store to the parking lot. "Most people live out there," he said. He pointed to the game. "I live in here." He tapped the glass of the screen.

Tibby was slightly unnerved by his honesty and the levelness of his stare. She had imagined she would be intimidating to a person like Brian.

"So tell us about *Dragon Master*," she asked, beginning to feel she was backing down.

"I'll show you," he said, slipping two quarters into the money slot. This was obviously why he'd agreed to this.

"Round one is the forest. The year is A.D. 436. The first great expedition in the search for the Holy Grail."

Tibby trained the camera on the screen, looking over his shoulder. The image wasn't as clear as she'd have liked, but it wasn't too bad.

"There are a total of twenty-eight rounds, spanning from the fifth century to the twenty-fifth century A.D. Only one person on this machine has ever gotten to round twenty-eight."

"You?" Tibby asked, a little breathlessly.

"Yeah, me," he said. "On February thirteenth."

Tibby the scornful documentarian knew this was excellent stuff. But for some reason, she felt mildly impressed in spite of herself. "Maybe you'll get there again today," she said.

"It's possible," Brian agreed. "Even if I don't, there's the whole world here."

Both Tibby and Bailey peered over his shoulder as Brian, a hugely muscular warrior, gathered troops of loyal men and a curvaceous woman to fight by his side.

"You don't even confront a dragon until level seven," he explained.

At level four, there was a sea battle. At level six, the vandals set fire to Brian's village, and he saved all the women and children. Tibby watched his hands, fast and sure on the various knobs and buttons. He never looked down at them.

Sometime after the second dragon appeared, Tibby heard the battery die and the camera flick off, but she kept watching.

After a long siege of a medieval castle, Brian paused the game and turned around.

"I think your battery ran out," he said.

"Oh, yeah. You're right," Tibby said nonchalantly. "That was my third one. I don't have another one charged. Maybe we could finish this later."

"Sure," Brian agreed.

"You can keep playing if you want," Tibby offered.

"I will," he said.

Bailey bought them each a Hostess fruit pie, and they watched the heroic version of Brian fight through twenty-four levels before being incinerated by dragon breath.

Eric was leading another run at five. Bridget wasn't sure he looked happy to see her.

"Today we're cutting our time to six-minute-fifty-second miles," Eric announced to the group. "Once again, you know your bodies. You know when you are overdoing it. It's hot out here. So take it easy. Slow down when you need to. This is conditioning, not competition." He looked right at Bridget.

"Ready?" he asked them after he'd given them a few minutes to stretch.

He seemed to resign himself quickly to the idea that Bridget was going to run alongside him no matter how fast or slow he ran. "You are quite a player, Bee," he said to her in a measured voice. "You put on a real show today." He thought she'd overdone it. That was obvious.

Bridget chewed the inside of her lip, ashamed. "I got too intense. I do that sometimes."

He made a face like that wasn't coming as a big surprise.

"I was showing off for you," she confessed.

He seemed to hold his thoughts for a second as he looked her right in the eyes. Then he looked back to see how close the next runner was. "Bee, don't," he said under his breath.

"Don't what?"

"Don't . . . don't . . . push this." He couldn't seem to find words he was happy with.

"Why not? Why am I not allowed to want you?"

He was taken aback by her directness. He glanced across at her and groaned. "Look, I'm . . . flattered. I'm honored. Who wouldn't be?"

Bridget clenched her jaws. *Flattered* and *honored* weren't the words she wanted to hear. Anyway, she didn't believe them.

He picked up the pace so they were a little farther ahead. "Bridget, you are beautiful. You are amazing and talented and just . . . just . . . irrepressible." His voice was softer now. He met her eyes. "It's not like I haven't noticed. Trust me, I have."

She felt hopeful now.

"But I'm a coach and you're . . . sixteen."

"So what?" she said.

"First of all it would be wrong, and second, it's completely against the rules."

Bridget tucked a stray strand of hair behind her ear. "Those aren't rules I care about."

Eric's face had closed off again. "I don't have a choice about them."

Though breakfast with Bapi had become a routine, it hadn't lost its awkwardness. Especially after what had happened.

This morning her Rice Krispies violently snapped, crackled, and popped while Bapi ate quiet Cheerios.

She studied him, searching for her moment. She tried to catch his gray-green eyes, similar in color to hers. She wanted to look sincere and repentant, but her noisy cereal was messing up the effect. The sight of the clumpy little stitches in his wrinkled skin gave her a pang of shame at the bottom of her stomach.

"Bapi, I . . ."

He looked up. His face was concerned.

"Well, I just . . ." Her voice was practically shaking. What was she thinking? Bapi didn't even speak English.

Bapi nodded and put his hand over hers. It was a sweet gesture. It meant love and protection, but it also meant, *We don't have to talk about it.*

She wished Effie weren't such a snoozer in the morning. Lena had been too tired and confused to come clean to Effie last night, and her grandparents hadn't discussed it at all. Effie had asked about the bandage on his cheek, but Bapi had shrugged it off, muttering in Greek. Now Lena wanted to tell her sister the whole story and at least get the patented Effie reality check, even if it was punishing. After that she'd tell Grandma, and then Grandma could explain it to Bapi. That would work better. But Effie was still asleep.

Upstairs after breakfast, Lena packed up her

painting supplies. Routine always helped an unsettled mind. She peered out her window at the time Kostos usually passed by to stop at the café up the street, before turning back downhill to the forge, but this morning he didn't. Of course he didn't.

Leaving the house, she decided to walk downhill today. Sunlight pulsing off the white walls beat into her eyes, casting clear light into her brain and illuminating its dusty, disregarded corners.

She walked toward Kostos's house. Because of the curve of the sidewalk, his house was positioned in such a way that if you happened to trip and roll, and the door to his house happened to be open, you could end up in his living room.

She walked by slowly. No sign of activity. Heading farther down the cliffside, she sent herself in the direction she believed the forge to be. Maybe she would pass him. Maybe she could talk to him or at least communicate by her facial expression that she knew things had gotten powerfully out of hand.

She didn't see him. She kept walking. Halfheartedly, she set up her easel just under her favorite church. She got out her charcoal, ready to scratch out the bones of the bell tower. Her hand hesitated as her mind raced around.

She put the charcoal away. Today, for a change, she didn't feel like spending quality time with Lena. She packed up the rest of her things and headed back uphill. Maybe she would pass by Kostos this time. Maybe she would go shopping with Effie, as Effie was always wanting to do, and buy one of those dumb olive-wood tourist bowls.

Maybe she would find a way to tell her grandmother what had really happened.

Well, she told herself on the bright side, Kostos wouldn't be bothering her anymore. But that side didn't seem so bright just now.

Carma,

We went hiking across this volcano field. Tres Virgenes, it's called. Quattro Virgenes and it could have been us. I swear I could smell the smoke, even though our guide said the volcanoes were inactive since last century.

Then we hiked down south through these canyons to look at ancient Indian rock art. First there were these hunting scenes, and then there was one big painting after another of these huge penises. Diana and I were laughing so hard we just sat on the ground. The coaches who came with us tried to shuttle us along. It was hilarious. I wish you could have been there.

Oh, the crazy pleasures of Baja.

Love,
Bee

Before you criticize someone, you should walk a mile in their shoes. That way, when you criticize them, you are a mile away from them, and you have their shoes.

—Frieda Norris

"Barbara, you know my daughter, Krista," Lydia said to the dressmaker on Tuesday afternoon.

Krista smiled delightfully.

Lydia gestured toward Carmen. "And this is my . . ." She paused. Carmen knew Lydia was working herself up to say stepdaughter, like Al called Krista, but she backed down. "This is Carmen."

"Lydia's my stepmother," Carmen clarified, just to be obnoxious.

Barbara wore her blond hair in a perfect bell-shaped bob. Her teeth, when she smiled, were a wall of white. Big and fake, Carmen concluded.

Barbara stared at Carmen. Carmen's hair was in a messy wad at the back. Her red tank top was soaked with sweat. "This is Albert's daughter?" she asked with obvious surprise, looking to Lydia instead of Carmen for verification.

"This is Albert's daughter," Carmen answered for herself.

Barbara wanted to backtrack. After all, Albert was paying the bills. "It's just that you . . . you must take after your mother," she said, as though that were diplomatic.

"I do," Carmen confirmed. "My mother is Puerto Rican. She speaks with an accent. She says a rosary."

Nobody seemed to pick up on her sauciness. The invisible girl.

"She has her father's aptitude for math," Lydia argued faintly, as though in her heart she didn't believe Carmen was related to Albert at all.

Carmen felt like smacking her.

"Well, let's get on with the fitting," Barbara suggested, setting an armful of plastic garment bags down on Lydia's bed. Lydia and Albert's bed. "Krista, let's try yours first."

"Oh, oh, can we look at Mama's first?" Krista begged. She literally pressed her hands together wistfully.

Carmen disappeared into an upholstered chair by the wall as Lydia proudly donned what looked to be at least seventy yards of shiny white fabric. Carmen thought it was frankly embarrassing for a woman over forty with two teenage children to wear a big puffy white thing at her wedding. The bodice was fitted, and the cap sleeves showed a whole lot of over-forty arm.

"Mama, you are gorgeous. You are a vision. I'm going to cry," Krista gushed without actually crying.

Carmen realized she was tapping her foot against the glassy wood floor, and she made herself stop.

Next, sweet, miniature, pale Krista tried on a pink-purple taffeta gown. Carmen could only pray her dress would not be identical to this one.

Krista's had to be taken in a little at the waist. "Oooh," said Krista, laughing, as Barbara cinched and pinned. The dress was heinous, but on colorless, curveless Krista it worked as well as it could.

Now it was Carmen's turn. Even though she was invisible, pulling the identical, stiff, shiny, too-small dress over her damp skin was miserable and humiliating. She couldn't look at anyone. She couldn't look at herself in the mirror. She didn't want the picture living in her memory for the rest of her life.

Barbara appraised her with critical eyes. "Oh my. Well, this is going to need some work." She went right to Carmen's hips and pulled the unfinished seams open. "Yes, we'll have to take this way out. I'm not sure I have enough fabric. I'll check when I get back to my office."

You are a horrible witch, Carmen thought.

She knew she looked absolutely awful in the dress. She was part Bourbon Street whore and part Latina first-communion spectacle.

Barbara examined the way the fabric stretched gracelessly across Carmen's chest. "We'll need to let that out too," she said, coming in close.

Carmen immediately crossed her arms. *Do not come near my breasts*, she ordered silently.

Barbara turned to Lydia in consternation, as though it were Carmen's fault that the stupid dress didn't fit. "I'm afraid I may have to start from scratch on this one."

"We should have given you Carmen's measurements ahead of time," Lydia confessed with some mortification. "But Albert wanted to wait until she got here to tell her about . . ." She trailed off, realizing she was heading into the land of tension.

"Usually a roughly constructed prototype works as a starting point," Barbara said, casting the blame back at Carmen and her butt.

"Carmen has to leave now," Carmen said to Barbara. Anger was swelling in her chest, squishing her heart, moving up into her throat. Her temper would not suffer one more second of Barbara.

"I hate this place," were Carmen's parting words to a confused Lydia. "And you should wear long sleeves." She stormed out of the room.

Paul surprised her by being in the hallway.

"You antagonize people," he murmured to the fast-moving Carmen. She was as much astonished by the four syllables in *antagonize* as by the meaning of his words.

You imagined that, she told herself, picking up her pace.

"Awesome pants," Bailey said, arriving at Wallman's at her regular time. Tibby had come to expect it. She didn't bother to complain anymore.

Tibby stood up from the low shelf where she'd been jabbing price stickers onto boxes of crayons. She looked down with open pride at the pants. "They are *the* Pants," Tibby explained. "They came yesterday." She had ripped open the package, covered with colorful, fake-looking stamps. She had held the Pants tightly, feeling like she was holding a part of Lena, and breathed in the smell of Greece that, she imagined, had seeped into the fabric. The Pants did smell faintly of olive oil—she wasn't imagining it. And there was a brownish spot on the front of the right leg, toward the upper thigh, that she figured must be Lena's grandfather's blood.

Bailey's eyes opened big, her face full of reverence. "They look fantastic on you," she said breathlessly.

"You should see them on my friends," Tibby said. More and more often, Bailey wanted to hear stories about Tibby's friends and updates from their letters. More and more Tibby felt like she was inventing an outside world for her and Bailey.

"Has anything happened *in* them yet?" Bailey asked, fully willing to believe in the magic of the Pants.

"Well, half in them, half out of them. A boy saw Lena naked, and her grandfather tried to punch him." Tibby couldn't help smiling at the thought. "If you knew Lena, you'd know this was a big problem."

"Lena's the one in Greece," Bailey said.

"Right."

"Has Bridget had the Pants yet?" Bailey asked. For some reason, Bailey was fascinated by Bridget.

"No, Carmen's next. Then Bridget."

"I wonder what Bridget will do in them," Bailey mused.

"Something insane," Tibby said lightly, but then she was quiet, regretting her choice of words.

Bailey studied her for a minute. "You worry about Bridget, I think."

Tibby was thoughtful. "Maybe I do," she considered slowly. "Maybe we all do a little."

"Because of her mom?"

"Yeah. A lot because of that."

"Was her mom sick?" Bailey pressed.

"Not sick . . . physically, exactly," Tibby said carefully. "She had . . . bad depression."

"Oh," Bailey said. She was willing to let the subject end there. She seemed to guess the rest.

"So . . . anything happen to you yet in the Pants?" Bailey asked.

"I spilled a Sprite, and Duncan accused me of receipt withholding."

Bailey smiled. "What's that?"

"I forgot to give a customer her receipt."

"Oh," Bailey said. "Bad."

"Hey, are you ready to head over to the Pavillion?" Tibby asked.

"Yeah. I brought the stuff. I charged all the batteries."

Bailey had started hanging out in Tibby's room, working on the movie while Tibby was at work. Tibby had taught Bailey the basics of editing and laying in the sound track on her iMac. Loretta always let Bailey in. It was kind of weird, but Tibby didn't mind anymore.

At the Pavillion, Margaret was still working the box office, so they had to wait. As soon as they walked into the lobby of the theater, Tibby spotted Tucker. She sucked in her breath. After the stories she'd heard about the places he went and the people he hung out with, she didn't expect to see him at the movie theater.

He was standing with two of his friends in the popcorn line. His arms were crossed, and he looked impatient.

"What do you see in that guy?" Bailey wondered aloud.

"Only that he's one of the best-looking guys I've ever seen in person," Tibby said. When he looked over and caught her eye, Tibby felt a surge of confidence when she remembered she was wearing the Pants. Then she felt a plunge in confidence when she realized she was still wearing the smock.

Would it be too obvious if she took this moment to wriggle out of her smock? Tucker finished buying his popcorn and a soda the size of a car battery and walked right up to her.

"Yo, Tibby. How's it goin'?" He was staring directly at her "Hi, I'm Tibby!" pin. He knew her name without the pin, but only because of her association with her hottie friends.

"Fine," Tibby said stiffly. She could never talk when she was around him.

She heard Bailey sniff derisively.

"You working at Wallman's?" Tucker asked. One of his friends smirked.

"No, she just wears the smock 'cause it's cool," Bailey snapped.

"See you," Tibby mumbled over her shoulder at Tucker. She dragged Bailey back out the door onto the heat of the sidewalk. "Bailey, keep your mouth shut, would you?"

Bailey had her feisty look. "Why should I?"

Margaret appeared from the box office. "Y'all ready?" she asked.

Tibby and Bailey glared at each other. "Yes, we're ready," Tibby said through tight jaws, feeling big.

"Margaret, how long have you worked here?" Tibby asked once they were set up in a quiet part of the lobby in front of a poster from *Clueless*— Margaret's choice.

"Lit's jist see." Margaret looked to the ceiling. "I giss it was . . . 1971."

Tibby swallowed hard. That was, like, thirty years ago. She looked closer at Margaret. She wore her blond hair in a high ponytail and wore a lot of eye shadow. She was obviously older than she looked, but Tibby had never dreamed she was *that* old.

"How many movies do you think you've seen?" Tibby asked.

"Over tin thousand, I would have to giss," Margaret said.

"And do you have one favorite?"

"I can't say, honestly," Margaret replied. "I have so minny. I luuuuved this one." She hooked her thumb at the movie poster behind her. She thought some more. "*Steel Magnolias* is one of my all-time best."

"Is it true you can recite whole scenes from movies?" Tibby asked.

Margaret blushed. "Sure. Well, I don't mean to brag or anything. I can only remember some parts. Right now there's this rill cute one with Sandra Bullock. You want to hear it?"

Margaret took off her pink cardigan, and Tibby noticed how small she was. She didn't look like she'd hit puberty, let alone crossed her fortieth birthday years ago.

What happened to you? Tibby wondered. She looked at Bailey. Bailey's mouth was very small in her face.

"Could we watch a movie with you?" Bailey asked.

Margaret's eyes were puzzled. "You mean jis go in and watch one now? All of us three together?"

"Yeah," Bailey said.

"Uh, I guess we could do that." Margaret's expression made a slow shift from doubt to interest. "There's that rill cute one jis startin' up in theater four."

Margaret followed Bailey and Tibby uncertainly down the dark aisle and into a middle row of seats. "I usually jis stand in the back," she explained in a whisper. "But these seats are rill nice, aren't they?"

As the fluffy plot progressed, Margaret looked

over at them so many times, checking excitedly for their reactions, that Tibby wondered, with a swelling sadness in her throat, how many of the ten thousand movies Margaret had watched with another person.

Bridget couldn't fall asleep. Even her spot at the edge of the beach under the stars felt stuffy and confining to her tonight. She felt a dangerous restlessness building up in her joints and muscles.

She got out of her sleeping bag and walked down to the water. It was gentle as ever. She wanted Eric to come to her. She wanted to be near him so badly.

She had an idea. She knew immediately it was a bad idea, but once it was there it was like a challenge. She couldn't not do it.

She walked quietly along the beach, hearing the hiss of sand between her feet. The far northern end of their little cove was even more desolate, and it was the place, she knew, where Eric shared a cabin with other coaches.

A memory popped into her head. It was something a psychiatrist had written about her in the months after her mother died. It was supposed to be confidential, but she found the report in her dad's desk drawer. "Bridget is single-minded in achieving her goals," Dr. Lambert had written. "Single-minded to the point of recklessness."

I'll just peek in, she promised herself. She couldn't very well stop now. She was right here. She found the door easily. The whole front of the cabin was open to the air. Inside were four beds. One was empty. Two others had sleeping trainers—college guys like Eric. In the fourth bed was unmistakably Eric. He was sleeping in a pair of boxers, his long frame sprawled out on the small bed. She took a step forward.

He must have sensed her there, because he jerked his head up suddenly. He put it back down on his pillow, then jerked it up again, realizing the significance of what he was seeing. He was alarmed that she was there.

She didn't say a word. She hadn't precisely meant to capture him this way. But obviously he was afraid she would say something. He got out of his bed and stumbled out of the cabin. He grabbed her hand and pulled her after him to a remote spot under a huddle of date palms.

"Bridget, what are you thinking?" He was groggy, disoriented. "You can't come here," he whispered.

"I'm sorry," she said. "I didn't mean to wake you up."

He blinked, trying to focus his eyes properly. "What *did* you mean?"

The wind blew her hair forward. The ends grazed his chest. She wished there were nerve endings in hair. She was wearing only a white T-shirt skimming the bottom of her underwear. It was awfully hard not to touch him. "I was thinking about you. I just wanted to see if you were asleep."

He didn't say anything and he didn't move. She put her two hands on his chest. In slow fascination she watched as he lifted his hand and put it to her hair, pushing it back from her face.

He was still sleepy. It was like this was the continuation of a dream. He wanted to fall back into this dream; she knew he did. She reached her arms around him and pressed her torso against his. "Mmmm," he rumbled.

She wanted to know the contours of his body. Hungrily she reached up to his shoulders, down over the heavy muscles of his upper arms. She reached up again to his neck, into his hair, down his chest, his hard stomach. That was when he seemed to wake up. He seemed to shake himself, seizing her upper arms and wrenching himself apart from her. "Jesus, Bridget." He groaned in loud, angry frustration. She took a step back. "What am I *doing*? You've got to get out of here."

He still held her arms, but more gently now.

He wasn't letting her have him, but he wasn't letting her go either. "Please don't do this. Please tell me you won't come back here." He searched her face. His eyes were begging her for different things at the same time.

"I think about you," she told him solemnly. "I think about being with you."

He closed his eyes and freed her arms. When he opened his eyes they were more resolute. "Bridget, go away now and promise me you won't do this again. I don't know if I'll be able to handle it."

She did go away, but she didn't promise anything.

Maybe he hadn't meant his words as an invitation. But that's how she took them.

Time tells the truth.

—Fortune cookie

"I want to sit here," Bailey declared, pulling a chair close to Mimi's box.

Seeing Mimi reminded her. "Oh, shit," Tibby mumbled.

"What?"

"I completely forgot to feed her yesterday," Tibby said, grabbing the canister of assorted seeds. She hadn't forgotten in months and months.

"Can I do it?" Bailey asked.

"Sure," Tibby said, not actually feeling sure. Nobody ever fed Mimi except for her. She had to walk herself across the room so she wouldn't micromanage.

Bailey finished feeding Mimi and sat down again.

"Ready?" Tibby asked, arranging the mike.

"I think so."

"Okay."

"Wait," Bailey said, standing up.

"Now what?" Tibby asked irritably. Bailey wanted to be interviewed for their movie. But now she was being weirdly uncertain about how she wanted it to go.

She was fidgety. Obviously she had an idea. "Can I wear the Pants?"

"The pants . . . *the* Pants?"

"Yeah. Can I borrow them?"

Tibby was doubtful. "First of all, I really don't think they'll fit you."

"I don't care," Bailey responded. "Can I try them? You don't have them for too much longer, do you?"

"Rrrrr." Impatiently Tibby retrieved them from her hiding place in her closet. She was terrified Loretta would throw them in the wash with a few cups of bleach, like she'd done with Tibby's wool sweaters. "Here." She handed them to Bailey.

Bailey slipped off her olive-green cargos. Tibby was struck by the whiteness of her skinny legs and the big, dark bruise that spread from her hip to her thigh.

"Ow, whadja do?" Tibby asked.

Bailey flashed her the "Don't ask, don't tell" look and pulled on the Pants. Magic though they were, they were too big for Bailey. She was tiny. Nonetheless she looked happy, and she hitched the wrinkly legs up over her feet.

"All good?" Tibby asked.

"All good," Bailey said, settling back into her chair.

Tibby held up the camera and pushed the On button. Through the lens, she could see Bailey a little differently. Her thin, almost transparent skin looked bruised and blue around her eyes. "So tell me things," Tibby said, not sure what Bailey wanted to cover, instinctively afraid of asking her direct questions.

Bailey pulled her bare feet up onto the chair, resting her arms on her bony knees and her chin on her forearm. Light slanted through the window and set her hair aglow.

"Ask me anything," Bailey challenged.

"What are you scared of?" The question got out of Tibby's mouth before she meant to ask it.

Bailey thought. "I'm afraid of time," she answered. She was brave, unflinching in the big Cyclops eye of the camera. There was nothing prissy or self-conscious about Bailey. "I mean, I'm afraid of not having enough time," she clarified. "Not enough time to understand people, how they really are, or to be understood myself. I'm afraid of the quick judgments and mistakes that everybody makes. You can't fix them without time. I'm afraid of seeing snapshots instead of movies."

Tibby looked at her in disbelief. She was struck by this new side of Bailey, this philosophical-beyond-her-years Bailey. Did cancer make you wise? Did those chemicals and X rays super-charge her twelve-year-old brain?

Tibby was shaking her head.

"What?" Bailey asked.

"Nothing. Just that you surprise me every day," Tibby said.

Bailey smiled at her. "I like that you let your-self be surprised."

Carma,

I'm writing from the post office, and this express mail costs more than what I make in two hours at Wallman's, so it better get to you tomorrow.

I can't figure out what the Pants meant to me yet. It was either profound or not. I'll tell you when I know.

You'll do better because you are the one and only Carma Carmeena.

I better sign off, 'cause the lady in the window is about to go postal (heh heh).

Love,
Tibby

Grandma looked stricken over lunch. She didn't want to talk about anything, she told them. Which turned out to mean that she didn't want to talk about anything Lena or Effie had to say. She was happy to listen to herself.

"I passed Rena this morning, and she didn't

speak to me. Can you imagine? Who does that voman tink she is?"

Lena moved the *tzadziki* around on her plate. One thing about Grandma: She was never too distressed to cook.

Bapi was attending to some business in Fira, and Effie was sending a million assorted looks to Lena across the table.

"Kostos has alvays been such a good boy, such a nice boy, but how do you ever know?" she mused.

Lena felt heartsick. Grandma loved Kostos. He was a bit of a creep, but he was obviously a huge source of pleasure in Grandma's life.

"Grandma," Lena broke in. "Maybe Kostos, maybe he—"

"Vhen you tink about the tings he's been trough, you vould tink he'd have troubles," Grandma went on, undeterred. "But I never saw them before."

"What kind of troubles?" Effie wanted to know.

"Grandma, maybe it didn't happen exactly like you thought it did," Lena tried out timidly, talking at the same time as Effie.

Grandma looked at the two of them wearily. "I don't vant to talk about it," she said.

As soon as an acceptable amount of food had been consumed, Effie and Lena quickly scrubbed their plates and then fled.

"What happened?" Effie demanded, less than a foot out of the house.

"Uhhhhh," Lena groaned.

"God, what is up with everybody?" Effie pressed.

Lena felt weary herself. "Listen, Ef, don't shout or scream or criticize until the end. Promise?"

Effie agreed. She mostly kept the promise until Lena got to the part about the fistfight, and then she couldn't contain herself anymore.

"No way! You are *not serious*! Bapi? Oh, my God."

Lena nodded.

"You better tell them all the truth before Kostos does, or you're going to feel like an idiot," Effie advised with her typical subtlety.

"I know," Lena said unhappily.

"Why didn't he just tell them all the truth at the time?" Effie wondered aloud.

"I don't know. There was so much confusion. I don't know if he even understood what the fight was about."

Effie shook her head. "Poor Kostos. He was so in love with you."

"Not anymore," Lena pointed out.

"Guess not."

BRIDGET: Hi, uh, Loretta?
LORETTA: Hello?

BRIDGET: Loretta, it's Bridget, Tibby's friend.
LORETTA: Hello?
BRIDGET (practically shouting): Bridget! It's Bridget. I'm calling for Tibby. Is she there?
LORETTA: Oh . . . Bridget?
BRIDGET: Yeah.
LORETTA: Tibby no home.
BRIDGET: Could you tell her I called? I don't have a number, so I'll have to call her back.
LORETTA: Hello?

When Carmen went downstairs shortly before dinner that night, she was ready for a fight. She was wearing the Pants, which gave her a feeling of remembering herself again. Remembering how she felt when people loved her. Remembering her skill for confrontation. She needed to bring the real Carmen downstairs and talk to her father and Lydia before she forgot herself and turned invisible again.

Lydia had certainly told him about the disastrous dress fitting and complained about her behavior. Carmen was ready to have it out. She'd love to shout at Lydia. She'd love to hear Lydia shout back. She needed that.

"Hi," Krista said from her homework station at the kitchen table. Carmen studied her for shades of meaning.

"Carmen, would you like a soda?" Lydia asked

brightly, measuring rice and pouring it into a pot.

Her dad appeared in the doorway, not yet changed out of his work clothes. "Hi, bun; how was your day?"

Carmen looked from her dad to Lydia in amazement. *My day was horrible!* she felt like shouting. *A dressmaker with fake teeth insulted and humiliated me. I acted like a brat.*

She didn't say that. Instead, she gaped at him in silence. Did he have any idea how she was feeling? How miserable she was here?

He wore his game face. So did Lydia. "Smells fantastic," he commented, keeping the scene on track.

"Roast chicken," Lydia supplied.

"Mmmmm," Krista said robotically.

Who were these people? What was the matter with them?

"I had an awful day," Carmen said, feeling her opportunity sliding away. She was too wretched to be a wiseass.

Her dad was already most of the way up the stairs, going up to change his clothes. Lydia pretended like she hadn't heard her.

Even in the Pants she was invisible. And mute. She strode dramatically out the front door and pulled it hard behind her. Luckily, the door still was capable of making a racket.

Of the thirty-six
ways of avoiding
disaster, running
away is best.
—Anonymous

Sometimes a walk helped cool Carmen's blood. Other times it didn't.

She marched all the way to the creek at the edge of the woods. She knew there were cottonmouths lurking in this dense place. She hoped one would bite her.

She pried a wide, heavy rock from the packed soil of the creek bank. She heaved it into the water, gratified by the big, sloppy splash that sent droplets of water onto her pants. The rock settled there in the creek bed, slightly obstructing the smooth way the water flowed. Her eyes stayed fixed on the rushing creek that dimpled around her rock. Within a few moments, the water seemed to adjust itself. It tucked the wide rock a little deeper into its bed and flowed smoothly again.

Dinner was definitely ready by now. Were they waiting for her? Were they wondering where she'd gone? Her father must have heard the door slam. Was he worried? Maybe her father had gone out looking for her. Maybe he'd walked north and sent Paul south to look for her along Radley Lane. Maybe Lydia's roast chicken was getting cold, but her father couldn't be bothered with that because Carmen was gone.

She started back toward the house. She didn't want her father to call the police out to look for her or anything. And Paul had just this morning gotten back from his visit with his dad. Paul had enough to think about.

She quickened her step. She was even a little bit hungry after not eating much of anything for days. "I eat when I'm happy," she'd mentioned to her father over her untouched plate of casserole the night before. He hadn't picked up on it.

Her heart was pounding as she made her way up the front steps, anticipating her father's face. Was he even there? Or out looking for her? She didn't really want to burst in if it was just Lydia and Krista.

She peered in the front door. The light was on in the kitchen, but the living room was dim. She crept around the side of the house to get a better look. It was dark enough outside that she wasn't worried about being spotted.

When she made her way to the big picture window that framed the dining room table she froze.

She stopped breathing. The anger was growing again. It grew up into her throat, where she could taste it, coppery like blood, in the back of her mouth. It grew down into her stomach, where it knotted her intestines. It made her arms stiffen and her shoulders lock. It pushed against her ribs until she felt they would snap like sticks.

Her father wasn't looking for her. He wasn't calling the police. He was sitting at the dining room table, with piles of roast chicken, rice, and carrots on his plate.

Apparently, it was time for grace. He held Paul's hand on one side and Krista's on the other. Lydia was directly across from him, her back to the window. The four of them made a tight cluster, their linked arms circling them like a garland, their heads bent, close and grateful.

A father, a mother, and two children. One bitter, mismatched girl standing outside, looking in, invisible. The anger was too big to hold inside.

She raced down the side steps and picked up two rocks, small and easy to grab. Motions were no longer connected to thoughts, but she must have climbed back up those steps and cocked her arm. The first rock bounced off the window frame. The second one must have shot right through the window, because she heard the glass shatter and she saw it sail past the back of Paul's head and smack the far wall, before it came to sit on the floor at her father's feet. She stayed long enough for her father to look up and see her through the jagged hole in the window and know that it was her and that he saw her and that she saw him, and that they both knew.

And then she ran.

Tibby,

I love outdoor showers. I love looking at the sky. I've even started going to the bathroom outside rather than close myself up in one of the sick outhouses. I'm a feral creature. Is that the word? You would hate all this crunchiness, Tib, but it is perfect for me. The thought of a shower under a ceiling makes me claustrophobic. Do you think anyone would notice if I started going to the bathroom in the backyard? Ha. Just kidding.

I think I wasn't made for houses.

Love,
Contemplative Bee

Lena got directions to the forge and a bag of pastries from the lady in the bakery. "*Antio*, beautiful Lena," the lady called. The town was small enough that all the locals now knew her as "shy and beautiful" Lena. "Shy" was the sympathetic interpretation she got from older people. "Snotty" was the unsympathetic one she got from people her own age.

From the bakery Lena walked herself to the forge, a low, detached brick building with a small yard at the front. Through the open double doors of the dark building she could see the blue-and-orange fire at the back. Was there seriously still a business in making horseshoes and boat fittings? She suddenly felt a kind of deep, twingy sorrow for Kostos and his grandfather. Kostos's bapi no doubt dreamed that his grandson would take over the family business and run it into the next century. But she also guessed that Kostos hadn't gotten himself accepted at the London School of Economics to spend his life as a blacksmith in a minuscule Greek village.

It was like how her father had become a respected lawyer in Washington, but her grandparents remained confounded that their son hadn't opened a restaurant. They were still sure he'd do it as soon as the moment was right. "He can always fall back on his cooking," Grandma said confidently whenever the subject of her son's profession came up. There was a mysterious chasm between this island and the greater world, just like there was between old and young, ancient and new.

Lena stood nervously at the opening to the yard. Kostos would be taking his lunch break anytime now. She crumpled the top of the paper bag in her sweaty hands. She felt oddly self-conscious about her appearance. She hadn't washed her hair this morning, so it probably looked kind of greasy at the top. Her nose was pink from sunburn.

Her pulse began to throb as soon as he appeared in the doorway. He looked sooty and old-fashioned in his dark clothes. His hair was disheveled from the protective gear he wore and his face was flushed and shining with perspiration. She trained her eyes on his. *Please look at me.* He didn't. He was too polite not to nod a little in acknowledgment of her when he walked by. But now it was his turn to ignore her and not give her any chance to communicate.

"Kostos!" she finally called out. He didn't answer. She didn't know whether he'd heard and ignored her, or whether she'd waited too long to speak.

Carmen ran on legs that didn't feel connected to her body. She ran all the way to the creek, jumped over the water, and settled down on the far bank. It occurred to her that her magical pants were going to get dirty, but the thought was squeezed out by a million other thoughts, and she let it float away. She looked up at the sky, lacy patterns of oak leaves cut out in black. She threw her arms to the sides as though she'd been crucified.

She lay there for a long time—some number of hours; she couldn't guess how many. She wanted to pray, but then she felt guilty because she only ever seemed to pray when she needed something. She wasn't sure she even wanted to alert God to her presence here: The Girl Who Only Prayed When She Needed Something. It might irritate Him. Maybe she should just hold out, and pray when it was just for the sake of praying so that maybe God would like her again. But God (sorry, God), who could ever remember to pray when things were just okeydokey? Good people, that was who. And she wasn't one of them.

By the time the moon peaked and had begun to fall, her anger had fully retreated into its normal place, and her brain had started working again.

Now that she was thinking, she thought that she had to go back home to Washington. But her thinking also informed her that she had left everything—her money, her debit card, her everything useful—in the house. Why was it that her temper and her thinking never happened at the same time? Her temper behaved like a glutton sitting in an expensive restaurant ordering a hundred dishes, only to disappear when the bill came due. It left her lucid mind to do dishes.

"You will not be invited back," she muttered to her temper, her evil twin, the bad Carmen.

Maybe she should just cede her body to her temper all the time. Let it deal with the consequences, instead of her rational, conscientious self, which ruled her body most of the time. Okay, some of the time.

The rational Carmen, poor sucker that she was, had to creep back into the sleeping house at three in the morning (The back door was open. Had somebody left it that way on purpose?) and collect her stuff in complete silence. Though the bad Carmen wished someone would hear her and confront her, the rational Carmen prevented her from making that wish come true.

Rational Carmen walked to the bus stop and slept on a bench until five o'clock, when the local buses started running again. She took a bus all the way downtown to the Greyhound station, where she used cash to buy a ticket for a bus to D.C. making no more than fifteen stops.

The rational Carmen had arrived in South Carolina, and the rational Carmen was leaving it. But she had made very few appearances in between.

She stared out the window as the bus ground through downtown Charleston, the sleeping apartment buildings, shops, and restaurants, hoping the alternate-universe Carmen with her fun, single dad was having a better time.

Bumble Bee,

I'm a mess. I can't even write about it yet. I just want to get this package off to you by the fastest, most expensive mail possible. But let me just say that the Pants have not caused me to behave like a decent and lovable person. I hope you do better with them. What do I hope? Hmmm . . . I hope these Pants bring you . . .

Courage? No, you have too much of that.

Energy? No, you have way too much of that.

Not love. You get and give loads as it is.

Okay, how 'bout this? I hope they bring you good sense.

That's boring, you're screaming at me, and I know it is. But let me tell you from recent experience, a little common sense is a good thing. And besides, you have every other charm in the universe, Bee.

Wear them well. XXXOOO

Carma

Life is so . . .
whatever.
—Kelly Marquette,
aka Skeletor

At breakfast, Bridget was thinking about sex. She was a virgin, as were her best friends. She'd gone out with a lot of different guys, usually within a larger pack of kids. She'd gone further than kissing with a couple of them but not very much further. She'd been driven more by curiosity than by physical yearning.

But for Eric, her body felt something else. Something bigger and craggier and stormier than she had glimpsed before. Her body wanted his in a painful, distinct, demanding way, but she wasn't even exactly sure what or how much it was asking for.

"What are you thinking about?" Diana asked, clinking her spoon against the bottom of her bowl.

"Sex," Bridget answered honestly.

"I could sort of guess that."

"Oh yeah?"

"Yeah. Does it have anything to do with where

you were last night?" Diana asked, curious but not pushy.

"Well, kind of," Bridget answered. "I did see Eric. But we didn't hook up or anything."

"Did you want to?" Diana asked.

Bridget nodded. "I think tonight might be the night." She tried to convey confidence without swagger.

"Tonight is going to be what night?" Ollie asked, sitting down with her tray.

"My night to hook up, Oh-livia," Bridget responded.

"You think so?" Olivia asked.

"I do." Bridget didn't want to go into what had happened last night. It seemed too intimate to give details.

"I can't wait to hear about it," Ollie said in a doubtful, challenging way.

Bridget couldn't resist a little bravado. "I can't wait to tell you."

Sherrie stopped by their table on her way out. "Bridget, you've got a package."

Bridget got up. A suspicion about the package sent a thrill up to her scalp. She was fairly sure the clothes she'd asked her dad for hadn't arrived yet. Her father was the notoriously cheap Dutchman. No way he would have sent her stuff by fast mail. That meant it was . . .

She ran barefoot to the main building and stood fidgeting at the telephone desk. "Hello!" she yelled to get attention. Patience might be a virtue, but it wasn't her virtue.

Eve Pollan, Connie's assistant, came out from the office. "Yeah?"

Bridget couldn't keep her feet still. "Package for me? Bridget Vreeland. V-R-E-E—"

"Here." Eve rolled her eyes. There was only one package on the shelf. She handed it over.

Bridget tore it apart right there. It was! It was the Pants. They were beautiful. She had missed them. They were already a little dirty, especially on the seat—somebody had been sitting on the ground in them. The thought made her laugh and ache for her friends at the same time. It really was like having a bit of Lena and Carmen and Tibby here. Although Carmen wouldn't be caught dead with mud stains on her butt. That had to have been Lena or Tibby. Bridget pulled the Pants on right over her white nylon shorts.

There was a letter too. She stuffed it in her pocket for later.

"Are these gorgeous pants or what?" she asked Eve, because sour Eve was the only one around.

Eve just looked at her.

Bridget ran back to the cabin for her cleats and her green jersey. Today was the first round of the Coyote

Cup championship. The Tacos were playing team five, the Sand Fleas. "Diana! Check these out!" Bridget commanded, wagging her butt in Diana's face.

"Are those the Traveling Pants?" Diana asked.

"Yeah! What do you think?"

Diana looked her over. "Well, they're jeans, pretty much. They fit you great, though."

Bridget beamed. She put on her cleats in a hurry and ran out to the field.

"Bridget, what are you thinking?" Molly demanded the minute she saw her.

"What do you mean?" Bridget asked, blinking innocently.

"You're wearing blue jeans. It's a hundred degrees out here. We're about to play our first real game."

"They're special pants," Bridget explained patiently. "They're kind of . . . magical. They'll make me play better."

Molly shook her head. "Bridget, you play plenty well without them. Take them off."

"Come on." Bridget tapped her cleat. "Please. *Please?*"

Molly dug in. "No." She couldn't help laughing. "You are a piece of work, girl."

"Rrrrr." Begrudgingly Bridget stripped off the jeans. She folded them carefully on the sidelines.

Molly put her arm around Bridget's shoulders before she sent them out into formation on the field.

"Play your game, Bee," she said. "But don't run away with it. Hear me?"

Bridget felt that Molly would make a good grandmother someday. It was too bad she was only twenty-three.

Bridget took off like a shot at the whistle, but she didn't run away with the game. She gave it to her teammates. She fed beautiful assists to them all game long. It was an act of sacrifice. She felt like Joan of Arc.

The Tacos were seeded first and the Fleas sixth, so it made sense they were beating them. But when they got up 12–zip, Molly called them over. "Okay, call off the cavalry, kids. Let's not be cruel." She glanced at Bridget. "Vreeland, take over for Rodman."

"What?" Bridget exploded. Brittany Rodman was the *goalie*. This was the thanks she got?

Molly made her "Don't mess with me" face.

"Fine," Bridget spat. She strode sullenly into the goal. She'd never played the position in her life.

Of course this was the moment Eric chose to come scouting. He couldn't help smiling at the sight of her, her hand planted on her stuck-out hip in the goal. She scowled at him. He scowled back. Sweetly, though.

She was busy making faces at him when a ball came flying at her. Her reflexes were good. She could hardly help herself. She snatched it out of the air.

When she saw the disappointment on all the faces, including Molly's, she threw the ball behind her, deep into the goal. Everyone burst into cheers. The long whistle ended the game. "To the Tacos, twelve to one," the ref called.

Bridget looked to Eric. He gave her a thumbs-up. She curtseyed.

The Pants were good luck, even from the side-lines.

"Carmen! Jesus! What are you doing here?"

Tibby was in her underwear and a T-shirt when Carmen burst into her room. Carmen had only stopped at home long enough to dump her suitcase and call her mom at work.

She threw herself at Tibby, nearly mowing her friend down. She slapped a kiss onto the side of Tibby's face and promptly started to cry.

"Oh, Carma," Tibby said, leading her friend over to her unmade bed and sitting her down.

Carmen really cried. She sobbed. She shuddered and heaved and gulped for breath like a four-year-old. Tibby put both arms around her, smelling and looking that comforting Tibby way, and Carmen was so relieved to be in a safe place with someone who knew her really, truly, that she let loose. She was the lost child in the department store, waiting until she was safe with her mother to cry a flood of tears.

"What? What? Was it so bad?" Tibby asked gently, when the volume and frequency of sobs had died down.

"It was horrible," Carmen wailed. "It was miserable."

"Tell me what happened," Tibby asked, her sometimes remote eyes damp and open with worry.

Carmen gave herself a few more breaths to calm down. "I threw a *rock* through the window while they were eating dinner."

This obviously wasn't what Tibby expected to hear. "You did? Why?"

"Because I hate them. Lydia, Krista." Pause. "Paul. Their whole stupid life," Carmen said sulkily.

"Right, but I mean, what happened that made you so upset?" Tibby asked, rubbing her back.

Carmen blinked. What a question. Where to begin? "They . . . they . . ." Carmen needed to stop and regroup. Why was Tibby interrogating her this way? Why wouldn't she just be regular and accept Carmen's feelings as proof that whatever was wrong was wrong? "Why are you asking so many questions? Don't you believe me?"

Tibby's eyes opened wider. "Of course I believe you. I'm just . . . trying to understand what happened."

Carmen bristled. "Here's what happened. I

went to South Carolina expecting to spend the summer with my dad. I show up and—surprise! He's moved in with a new family. Two kids, nice big house, the works."

"Carmen, I know all that. I read your letters. I promise."

For the first time Carmen observed that Tibby looked tired. Not just stayed-up-too-late tired, but tired on the inside. Her freckles stood out against white skin on her nose and cheeks.

"I know. Sorry," Carmen said quickly. She didn't want to fight with Tibby. She needed Tibby to love her. "Is everything okay with you?"

"Oh, yeah. Fine. Weird. Good. I guess."

"How's Wallman's?"

Tibby shrugged. "Mostly despair. As usual."

Carmen gestured toward the guinea pig cage. "How's the rat?"

"Mimi's fine."

Carmen stood and hugged Tibby again. "I'm sorry for putting on the drama class. I'm so happy to see you. I've just wanted so much to spill to you, I can't even make any sense."

"No, it's okay," Tibby said, squeezing Carmen back hard, then sitting on the bed. "Just tell me everything that happened, and I'll tell you you're good and that the rest of them suck," she promised, sounding more like her usual self.

I'm not good were the words that bubbled to the surface, but Carmen kept them in her mouth. She sighed and lay back on Tibby's bed. The wool blanket was itchy. "I guess I just felt . . . *invisible* there," she answered slowly, thoughtfully. "Nobody paid any attention to me. Nobody listened when I said I was unhappy or complained when I acted like a brat. They just want everything to look and seem perfect."

"'They' is Lydia mostly? Your dad?" Tibby let the last word linger.

"Yeah. Lydia mostly."

"Are you feeling mad at your dad too?" Tibby asked carefully.

Carmen sat up. Why couldn't Tibby just get mad with her? Tibby was the master of anger. She judged without reason; she loathed on a dime. She hated your enemies more than you did. "No I'm not! I'm mad at those other people!" Carmen shot back. "I don't want to have anything to do with them. I want them to go away and for it just to be me and my dad again."

Tibby backed away a little. Her eyes seemed wary. "Carma, do you think . . . I mean, is it really . . ." Tibby pulled her feet up onto the bed. "Is it possible it's not the worst thing in the world?" she asked, looking down. "I mean, compared to the really bad things?"

Carmen gaped at her friend. When had Tibby become Miss Perspective? Miss Proportion? If anybody got feeling sorry for herself and blaming other people for it, it was Tibby. Why was Tibby making her be reasonable when she just needed to be heard?

"Where'd ya put Tibby?" Carmen finally asked with a punctured lung and walked out of the room.

Dear Lena,

So the movie is going along, but it isn't how I expected. Bailey has become my self-appointed assistant. I let her do the interview with Duncan, Assistant General Manager of the World. It didn't come out funny, like I'd planned. But it was kind of cool anyway. The people I find most laughably insane, she seems to find most interesting.

So how's the boxing Bapi? How's ineffable Eff? Don't torture yourself, Len. We love you too much.

Tibby

That afternoon was their match against the Gray Whales. Meanwhile, Los Cocos, Eric's team, won their first match too. They were playing against team six, the Boneheads, tomorrow. Then the grand all-Coyote championship match was planned for the day after. Bridget took it for granted that the Tacos would be playing in the finals.

They waited for six o'clock, for the sun to sink and the air to cool to start the game. The whole camp was watching this time. The light was pink and pretty, slanting across the field. Bridget watched Eric sitting on the ground with a couple of other people on a checked blanket, laughing at something Marci said. Jealousy stabbed through her heart. She didn't want other girls making him laugh.

She'd brought the Pants with her again. She carefully folded them on the sidelines.

Molly was regarding her. Bridget didn't like the look on her face. Was Molly going to play her at goalie the whole game? "Bridget. You play defense."

"What? No way."

"Yes way. Get out there. Don't go past midfield," Molly added bossily, like Bridget had never watched a soccer game in her life.

"Go, Bridget!" Diana yelled from the sidelines. She was kicking back on the grass with a bunch of other girls, eating chips and salsa.

Bridget lined up at defense. She toiled back there all game long as Ollie and Jo and other girls played for glory. At least Bridget could feel good about destroying the Whales' offense.

By the middle of the second half it was 3–0. Bridget saw her chance. It was too good to pass up. There was a big skirmish on the sidelines, drawing nearly everybody from their positions. Bridget found herself drawn up to midfield with the far half of the field almost completely open.

Ollie had the inbounds pass and spotted Bridget in the corner of her eye. Making sure she stood behind the midfield line, Bridget efficiently captured the ball and sent it in a high, fast arc toward the goal. The crowd grew quiet. Everybody's eyes were on the ball. The goalie reached high and jumped. The ball sailed up and over her, sinking into the corner of the net.

Bridget looked directly at Molly. She was the only person on the sidelines who wasn't cheering.

"Bee, Bee, Bee!" Diana and her friends were chanting.

After that, Molly took Bridget out of the game. Bridget faintly wondered whether she would be asked back here next year. She sat on the grass and ate chips and salsa, enjoying the burning sensation in her mouth and the last rays of the sun on her shoulders.

You will make all
kinds of mistakes:
but as long as you
are generous and true
and also fierce you
cannot hurt the world
or even seriously
distress her.
—Winston Churchill

Lena needed to get back to painting. She was just hanging around, day after day, wanting to see Kostos, waiting for him to please return her glance, waiting to discover that he'd told everybody what happened between them—almost wanting him to. Half the time she believed herself that she couldn't find any way to make her stony, impassive grandparents talk about it. Half the time she knew she was lying the other half of the time. She was making excuses for her own discomfort.

She couldn't drink another coffee with Effie at the place with the cute waiter. She couldn't spend another afternoon on the scorching black sand at Kamari beach. She couldn't take yet another fruitless walk past the Dounas place and down to the forge. It was pitiful, was what it was. She needed to get back to painting.

She'd return to her olive trees by the pond. Of all

the paintings she'd ever done, the olive tree painting was her favorite. It was a little smeared, but it had mostly survived her temper tantrum. Today she packed a hat and a bathing suit. Just in case. She felt brave going back there. It didn't take much to make her feel brave.

The walk uphill felt even steeper than it had been nine days ago; the transformation from rock to meadow seemed even more dramatic. She felt an extra kick in her blood flow when the picturesque little grove came into sight. She went to the exact spot she'd been before. She could practically see the three holes her easel had made in the ground. Carefully she set up her panel and squeezed fresh blobs of paint onto her palette. She loved the smell of her paints. This was good.

She mixed the precise shade of silver, brown for warmth, green, and blue — those olive tree leaves wanted more blue than you would imagine. Each one seemed to reflect a tiny piece of the sky. The slow hypnosis of deep concentration was passing over her. It was her safest feeling, a state she preferred to stay in far longer than most human beings. She was like one of those strange hibernating frogs whose hearts didn't beat for a whole winter. She liked it that way.

She heard a splash. She looked up, trying to pull her senses back to alertness. She blinked, forcing her eyes to see three dimensions as three dimensions again. There was another splash. Was someone swimming in the pond?

There were few sensations Lena hated more than thinking she had perfect privacy and discovering she didn't.

She took a few steps away from her easel and peered around a tree to give herself a partial glimpse of the pond. She discerned a head. A person's head. From the back. A surge of frustration gripped her jaw. She wanted this to be her place. Why couldn't people just leave it alone?

She probably should have left at that exact moment. Instead she took two steps forward and gave herself a better view. The better view turned its head and suddenly wore the face of Kostos. At that moment he saw her gaping at him in the shallow pond.

This time he was naked and she was clothed, but like last time, she was the one shrinking and blushing and he was the one calmly standing there.

Last time she had been mad at him. This time she was mad at herself. Last time she had thought he was a vain, presumptuous jerk, but this time she knew she was. Last time she had dwelled obsessively on her own exposed body; this time she was thinking about his.

Last time he hadn't been spying on her. Last time he hadn't followed her. He was probably as shocked to see her as she was to see him.

Before now she thought he'd barged into her special place. Now she knew she had barged into his.

Lena,

I have a feeling this is going to be a big night. I don't know what's going to happen, but I have the Pants, which feels a little like having you and Tib and Carmen, so it can't be bad.

I'm missing you all so much now. It's been almost seven weeks. Eat a piece of spanakopita for me, okay?

Bee

Bridget crawled into her sleeping bag in the Pants and a tank top. It was a part of the magic of the Pants that they felt loose and airy in this heat. She suspected they would feel snug and protective in colder air.

She couldn't sleep, of course. She couldn't lie there either. Her legs refused to stay still. If she walked around camp, she knew she might get busted before she'd even gotten to do anything truly bad. Instead she walked out onto the headlands. She sat on a rock, pushed the cuffs of the Pants up to her knees, and dangled her feet in the water. Suddenly she wished she had a fishing rod.

She remembered the place she and her brother

used to go on the eastern shore of the Chesapeake when she was little. They went fishing every day. It was the only outdoorsy thing she could remember him doing. Each day, he'd keep his best fish. He learned to clean and gut them. Each day, she'd throw all of hers back. Long after that, with a pang of remorse, she pictured every fish in the Wye River with a hole in its lip.

She couldn't picture her mother there, although she knew she was. Maybe she was in one of her tired periods, staying in bed all day with the shutters closed to protect her eyes.

Bridget yawned. The frantic energy was seeping out of her limbs, leaving a deep physical exhaustion. Maybe she should just go to sleep tonight, leave this adventure for tomorrow.

Or she could go to him right now. Again, the thought was a challenge. She couldn't ignore it. *I think, therefore I do.* The hum of excitement started again in her feet, cramping her overworked calves.

All lights were off. It was late enough now. She looked back at her lone sleeping bag on the beach. She tiptoed back along the slippery rocks.

Was he waiting for her? He would be furious. Or he would succumb. Or some combination of the two.

She was pushing him, she knew. She was pushing herself. It was hard to stop.

Like a ghost, she glided silently past his door.

He wasn't asleep. He was sitting up. He saw her and got out of bed. She hopped off the small porch and walked through the palm trees to the wooded edge of the beach. He followed her shirtless, in his boxer shorts. He didn't have to follow her.

Her heart purred. She reached for him. "Did you know I would come?" she asked.

She could barely make out his features in the darkness. "I didn't want you to come," he said. He paused for a long time. "I hoped you would."

In most of Bridget's romantic fantasies, her imagination toyed elaborately with the setup, fast-forwarding and rewinding, rewinding, rewinding. In her imagination, Bridget had gotten herself to that wrenching first kiss again and again, in ever more perfect ways. But she hadn't gotten beyond that.

Long after she'd left Eric, she lay in her sleeping bag. She shivered. Her eyes were full. They dripped. From sadness, or strangeness, or love. They were the kind of tears that came when she was just too full. She needed to make a little room. She stared at the sky. It was bigger tonight. Tonight her thoughts roamed out into it, and like Diana had said, they didn't find anything to bounce off. They just went and went until nothing felt real. Not even the thoughts. Not even thinking itself.

She had clung to him, wanting him, unsure, brazen, and afraid. There was a storm in her body, and when the storm got too strong, she got out. She floated up to the palm fronds. She'd done it before. She'd let the ship go down without its captain.

The intimacy between them had been unfathomable. It now stayed there with her, wobbly, waiting to be taken care of. She didn't know how to do that.

Bridget pulled her thoughts back in, coiling them like a kite string.

Carefully she rolled her sleeping bag under her arm and crept back into the cabin. She lay down, her back flat on the bed. Tonight she would let her thoughts stray no farther than the weathered planks.

Tibby,

I feel like such an idiot. I was vain enough to think Kostos was so in love with me he couldn't resist following me and spying on me at the pond. Then I went back to the same place and saw him swimming there. Yes, naked. He probably swims there every summer afternoon, and here I thought he was following me.

One other thing, which was easy to miss what with him being naked (Oh. My. God.) and all the screaming (me) and acting like an idiot (also me). But guess

227

what? Kostos looked right into my eyes. Finally, after all these days, he looked at me.

If you were here, you would make me laugh about this. I wish you were.

Love,
Lena

P.S. Have you heard from Bee recently?

The phone rang. Carmen checked the caller ID panel, knowing it wasn't for her. Who was going to call her? Tibby? Lydia? Krista maybe? It was her mom's boss. It was always her mom's boss. Carmen's mother was a legal secretary, and her boss seemed to think Carmen's mom was his baby-sitter.

"Is Christina there?" Mr. Brattle asked in his usual hurried way.

Carmen checked the wall clock over the refrigerator. It was ten fourteen. Why should he be calling at ten fourteen? Once again he'd lost a memo, or hit the wrong button on his computer or forgotten how to tie his shoes. "She's visiting Grandma in the hospital. She's very ill," Carmen said pitifully, even though her mother was upstairs watching television and her grandma would probably outlive her grandchildren. Carmen liked to make Mr. Brattle feel either embarrassed or guilty for calling. "She should be back by midnight. I'll ask her to call you then."

"No, no," Mr. Brattle blustered. "I'll speak with her tomorrow."

"Okay." Carmen went back to her food. The only good thing about Mr. Brattle was that he paid her mother a ton of money and never dared refuse her a raise. It was fear, not generosity, Carmen suspected, but who was she to question it?

She'd laid out four possible snacks on the kitchen table. A tangerine, a bag of Goldfish crackers, a hunk of cheddar cheese, a bag of dried apricots. The theme tonight was orange.

Not one thing she'd put in her mouth had tasted good in the almost two weeks since she'd been home from South Carolina. She had hardly eaten a bite of dinner, and now she was hungry. Hmm. She went for the dried apricots and chose one from the bag. The skin was soft, but the apricot was tough when she put it in her mouth. Suddenly she had the acute sensation that she was chewing on somebody's ear. She spit it into the garbage and put everything else away.

She went upstairs and peered into her mother's room. An old *Friends* episode was on the TV. "Hi, sweet. You want to watch with me? Ross fooled around on Rachel."

Carmen slouched down the hall. Mothers were not supposed to care about Ross or Rachel. Carmen had liked the show before her mom started watching it in reruns. She flopped onto her bed. She had to cover her head with a pillow when her mother's loud laugh tore a hole in the wall.

Carmen had sworn to herself she was not going to be bothered by her mom. She was not going to be irritable and complaining. No sighing, no eye-rolling. She had to be loved by at least one of her parents. It was an easy promise to make when Carmen was alone. But when she was faced with her actual mother, it became impossible to keep. Her mom was always doing something unforgivable like laughing too loud at *Friends* or calling her computer her "Vaio."

Carmen sat up in bed and eyed the wall calendar. Even though she hadn't marked the day of her father's wedding, it seemed to jump out at her. Only three more weeks. Did her dad even care that she wouldn't be there?

Her dad had called her mother briefly the day Carmen left South Carolina to confirm that she was safely home. He'd called again a week ago to talk to Christina about some money thing having to do with Carmen's dental insurance. She couldn't believe how many things the two of them found to say about "deductibles." He hadn't asked to talk to Carmen.

Carmen could have called him, of course. She could have apologized or at least offered some explanation. She hadn't.

Guilt, like the cat she'd never had, wove around

her legs and hopped up onto the bed to insinuate itself at close range. "Go away," she said to the guilt. She imagined it brushing alongside her, swiping its tail against her cheek. Guilt wanted her most when she least wanted it. Cats always loved people who were allergic to them.

She wouldn't hold it. No way. She'd put it outside and let it screech all it wanted.

Unbidden, the picture of her father's face through the broken window barged into her mind. He was more than surprised. He simply couldn't process what he saw. He thought Carmen was better than that.

"All right, come on up." The guilt made muffins on her stomach and curled in for a long stay.

Wish for what you
want.
Work for what you
need.
—Carmen's
grandmother

"So guess what?" Effie's cheeks were deeply flushed, and her feet were working a miniature Riverdance on the tile floor.

"What?" Lena asked, looking up from her book.

"I kissed him."

"Who?"

"The waiter!" Effie practically screamed.

"The waiter?"

"The waiter! Oh my God! Greek boys make out better than American boys!" Effie declared.

Lena could not believe her sister. She could not believe she and Effie came from the same parents. Obviously they hadn't. One of them was adopted. Seeing that Effie looked identical to their parents, that left Lena. Maybe she was Bapi's illegitimate love child. Maybe she really had been born on Santorini.

"Effie, you made out with him? What about Gavin? You know, your boyfriend?"

Effie shrugged blithely. Her happiness made her impervious to guilt. "You're the one who said Gavin smelled like pork rinds."

It was true. "But Effie, you don't even know this guy's name! Did you call him 'the waiter' to his face? Isn't that kind of tacky?"

"I know his name," Effie said, undisturbed. "It's Andreas. He's seventeen."

"Seventeen! Effie, you're fourteen," Lena pointed out. She sounded, even to herself, like the principal of a very strict school.

"So? Kostos is eighteen."

Now Lena's cheeks were just as red. "Well, I didn't make out with Kostos," she sputtered.

"That was your fault," Effie said, and she walked out the door.

Lena threw her book on the floor. She wasn't actually reading it anyway. She was too miserable, too preoccupied.

Effie was fourteen, and she'd kissed many more boys than Lena had. Lena was supposed to be the pretty one, but Effie was always the one with the boyfriend. Effie would grow up to be the happy old woman with the big family, surrounded by people who loved her, and Lena would be the weird, scrawny maiden aunt who was invited over only because they felt sorry for her.

She took out her drawing stuff and set it up,

looking at the view out her window. But when she put her nubby piece of charcoal to her paper, her fingers didn't make a horizon line. Instead they drew the contour of a cheek. Then a neck. Then an eyebrow. Then a jaw. Then a hint of shadow on that jaw.

Her hand was flying. She was drawing much more loosely than usual. A hairline like . . . that. A nostril like . . . that. An earlobe like . . . She closed her eyes, remembering the exact shape of his earlobe. She seemed to stop breathing. Her heart stopped beating. Rough lines of his shoulders fell off at the bottom of the paper. Now his mouth. The mouth was always the hardest. She closed her eyes. His mouth . . .

When she opened them she imagined she saw the real Kostos standing beneath her window. Then she realized it *was* the real Kostos standing beneath her window. He looked up. She looked down. Could he see her? Could he see her drawing? Oh no.

Her heart started up again with a jolt. It took off in a flat-out sprint. She vaguely wondered whether hibernating frogs' hearts beat twice as fast in the summertime.

Girls who were friends last night were vultures this morning.

"So what happened?" Ollie wanted to know, landing on Bridget's bed before her eyes were fully open.

Diana was getting dressed. She came over

when she saw Bridget was at least partly awake.

Even Emily and Rosie migrated over. Girls who wouldn't take risks both loved and hated girls who did.

Bridget sat up. Last night was slow coming back. In sleep she'd gone back to being the yesterday Bridget.

She looked at them, their eyes curious — even hungry.

Bridget had seen too many movies. She hadn't imagined her encounter with Eric would be . . . personal. She thought it would be a jaunt. An adventure to brag to her friends about. She expected to feel powerful. In the end she didn't. She felt like she'd scrubbed her heart with SOS pads.

"Come on," Ollie pressed. "Tell us."

"Bridget?" It was Diana.

Bridget's voice was buried deep this morning rather than sharp on her tongue. "N-Nothing," she managed. "Nothing happened."

Bridget could see Ollie reappraising the ghosty look in her eyes. So it wasn't sex; it was disappointment.

Diana's eyes said she was unsure. Her intuition was telling her something else. But she wasn't distrustful. She waited until the others were drifting away. She touched Bridget's shoulder. "You okay, Bee?"

Her kindness made Bridget want to cry. She couldn't talk about this. Nor could she look at Diana if she wanted to keep it to herself. "I'm tired today," she told her sleeping bag.

"Do you want me to bring you something from breakfast?"

"No, I'll come in a few minutes," she answered.

She was glad when they were all gone. She curled back up and fell asleep.

Later, Sherrie, one of the camp staffers, came to check on her. "Are you feeling okay?" she asked Bridget.

Bridget nodded, but she didn't emerge from her sleeping bag.

"The Cocos and the Boneheads are playing in the semis in a couple of minutes. Do you want to watch?"

"I'd rather sleep," Bridget said. "I'm tired today."

"Okay." Sherrie turned to go. "I wondered when that energy was going to run out."

Diana, who returned a couple of hours later, told Bridget that the Cocos had crushed the Boneheads. It would be a Taco/Coco final.

"Are you coming to lunch?" Diana asked. She kept her tone light, but her eyes showed her concern.

"Maybe in a little while," Bridget answered.

Diana cocked her head. "Come on, Bee, get out of bed. What's with you?"

Bridget couldn't begin to explain what was with

her. She needed somebody to explain it to her. "I'm tired," she said. "Sometimes I just need to catch up on sleep. Sometimes I crash for a whole day."

Diana nodded, as though reassured that this was just another part of the peculiar Bridget canon.

"Can I bring you something? You must be starving."

Bridget had earned her reputation as a rapacious eater. But she wasn't hungry. She shook her head.

Diana considered all this. "It's weird. In almost seven weeks I've never seen you under a roof for more than three minutes. I've never seen you stay still except when you were asleep. I've *never* seen you miss a meal."

Bridget shrugged. "I contain multitudes," she said. She thought it was from a poem, but she wasn't sure. Her father loved poetry. He used to read it to her when she was little. She could sit still better back then.

Dad,
    Please accept this money to fix the broken window. I'm sure it's already fixed, considering Lydia's house pride and her phobia about un-air-conditioned air, but

Dear Al,
    I can't begin to explain my actions at

Lydia's—I mean yours and Lydia's house.
When I got to Charleston, I never imagined
that you would have

Dear Dad and Lydia,
    I apologize to both of you for my irra-
tional behavior. I know it's all my fault, but
if you would have listened to ONE THING I
had to say, I might not have

Dear Dad's new family,
    I hope you'll all be very happy being blond
together. May people speak only in inside voices for the rest of your lives.
P.S. Lydia, your wedding dress makes your
arms look fat.

Carmen opened the padded envelope and
shoved in all her cash. One hundred eighty-seven
dollars. She considered putting in the ninety cents
in change, but it seemed like something a seven-
year-old in an after-school special would do. And
besides, it would probably cost more postage to
send coins than the coins were worth. That
thought stimulated her math-geek brain.
    She stapled the envelope closed without
including a note and carefully wrote out the
address and return address, then hustled out the

door to get to the post office before it closed. Who was her mom to complain that she loafed around the house with nothing to do?

On a sweltering afternoon, Lena was lying on her back on the tile floor, staring at the ceiling and thinking about Bridget. Bridget's last letter worried her. Bee followed her heart with such manic abandon sometimes, it scared Lena. Usually Bee sailed along in triumph and glory, but once in a while she crashed on the rocks.

For some reason Lena thought of a dream she'd had. In it, she was a small house with whitewashed knuckles clinging to the side of the cliff. She knew she had to hold on tight, because it was a long drop into the cauldron below. A part of her wanted to release those cramped fingers and just fall, but another part of her warned that you couldn't just fall for the thrill of it.

Grandma was sitting on the sofa, sewing something. Effie was off somewhere. Lena would have bet her paints her sister was making out with the waiter.

For some reason, thinking about Bridget or maybe the dream, or maybe it was the heat, put Lena in a funny, free-associating kind of mood. "Grandma, why does Kostos live with his grandparents?"

Grandma sighed. Then, to Lena's surprise, she

started to answer. "It's a sad story, lamb. Are you sure you vant to know it?"

Lena wasn't totally sure. Grandma went on anyway.

"Kostos's parents moved to the United States, like so many young people," she explained. "He vas born there."

"Kostos is a U.S. citizen?" Lena asked.

Lena was too hot to turn her head, but she did anyway. Grandma nodded.

"Where did they live?"

"New York City."

"Oh," Lena said.

"His parents had Kostos, then another little boy two years later."

Lena was beginning to guess how sad this story was going to be.

"When Kostos vas three years old, the whole family vas driving to the mountains in the vintertime. There vas a terrible car wreck. Kostos lost both his parents and his baby brother."

Grandma paused, and Lena felt, even in 115-degree heat, shivery bumps rise over the length of her body.

When Grandma started up again, Lena could hear the emotion in her voice. "They sent little Kostos back here to his grandparents. It vas the best idea at the time."

Grandma was in a strange mood, Lena observed. She was unusually relaxed, reflective, full of old sorrow. "He grew up here as a Greek boy. And ve all loved him. The whole town of Oia raised him."

"Hey, Grandma?"

"Yes, lamb?"

This was her moment. She didn't let herself think long enough to chicken out. "You know that Kostos never hurt me. He never touched me or did anything wrong. He is just the boy you think he is."

Grandma let out a long breath. She put her sewing down and settled herself back on the sofa. "I tink I knew that. After some time passed, I tink I knew that."

"I'm sorry I didn't say anything before," Lena said solemnly, filled with equal parts relief at having finally said it and sadness that it had taken her this long.

"In some vay, maybe you did try to tell me," Grandma noted philosophically.

"Will you tell Bapi what I just said?" Lena asked.

"I tink he already knows."

Lena's throat now felt painfully tight. She turned over from her back to her side, away from Grandma, and let her eyelids shut to release her tears.

She was sad about what had happened to Kostos. And someplace under that, she was sad that people like Bee and Kostos, who had lost everything, were still open to love, and she, who'd lost nothing, was not.

My karma ran over
my dogma.
—Bumper Sticker

Bridget moved herself out to the little porch of her cabin. She could look at the bay at least. She had a pen and a pad of paper. She needed to send the Pants off to Carmen, but today was a hard day for writing.

She was sitting there, chewing on her pen cap, when Eric came over. He sat on the railing.

"How's it going?" he asked.

"Fine," she said.

"You missed the game," he said. He didn't touch her. He didn't look at her. "It was a good one. Diana tore up the field."

They were rewinding the clock. He was back to being the benign coach, and she was the irrepressible camper. He was asking her permission to pretend that whatever had happened didn't happen.

She wasn't sure she wanted to give it. "I was tired. Big night last night."

His face colored. He held out his hands and looked at his palms. "Listen, Bridget." He seemed to be picking over a very paltry assortment of phrases. "I should have sent you away last night. I shouldn't have followed you when I saw you pass by my door. . . . I was wrong. I take responsibility."

"It was my choice to come." How dare he take her power?

"But I'm older than you. I'm the one who . . . I'm the one who would get in serious shit if people found out."

He still wouldn't look at her. He didn't know what else to say. He wanted to leave. She could see that clearly. "I'm sorry," he said.

She threw her pen after him. She hated that he'd said that.

Carmen,
    Here are the Pants. I'm very mixed up. If I had listened to your advice about good sense, I wouldn't be like this.
    So right back at you. Good sense rules. I wish I had some.

Love,
Bee

"Tibby, turn the camera off."
"Please, Carma? Please?"

"Can you put on the Pants for the interview?" Bailey asked.

Carmen gave her a look of full disdain. "I'm not doing an interview. What are you guys, the Coen brothers?" she snapped.

"Carmen, just be quiet and cooperate for once in your life." Tibby said it in a way that was irritable but not mean, if that was possible.

You antagonize people, Carmen reminded herself. *You will grow up to be old and bitter. You will wear lipstick way outside the lines and shout at children in restaurants.*

"Fine," she said. She changed into the Pants, then sat and studied Bailey as she started to get her camera equipment in order. The girl was dressed almost exactly the same way as Tibby. She was mini-Tibby with a mike and a boom. Her purple undereye circles even matched Tibby's. Carmen briefly wondered why Tibby was hanging around with a twelve-year-old, but whatever. It wasn't Tibby's fault all her friends had gone away.

The room got quiet. Tibby fiddled with the lights. Both moviemakers got deadly serious. She heard Bailey gasbagging into the mike like Dan Rather minus the testicles. "Carmen Lowell is Tibby's beloved friend from when they were . . ."

This was making Carmen uncomfortable. "Um . . . you know, Tibby and I are fighting right now."

Tibby cut the camera. Bailey looked up in irritation. She batted the fight away with a flick of her wrist. "You love each other. Tibby loves you. It doesn't matter."

Carmen glared at her in disbelief. "Hello? You're twelve."

"So? I'm still right," Bailey shot back.

"Can we get back to work?" Tibby asked.

Since when had Tibby developed the work ethic of a Pilgrim?

"I'm just saying, it feels weird to go on without mentioning that you and I had a huge fight, Tibby," Carmen said.

"Fine, you mentioned it," Tibby said.

Most people avoided conflict. Carmen was beginning to worry that she craved it like an addict. *You antagonize people*, she reminded herself. She shoved her hands into her pockets, fingering the grains of sand that were caught in the lining there.

"I'm going to ask the questions," Bailey said. "You just be yourself."

How had the modern world created such a confident twelve-year-old? Somebody ought to fill her in on that Ophelia syndrome right away. "Fine," Carmen said. "Am I supposed to look at the camera?"

"If you want to, you can," Bailey replied.

"Okay."

"Ready to go?"

"Ready."

Sitting on her neatly made bed, Carmen crossed her legs.

"So Tibby tells me your father is getting remarried this summer," Bailey started.

Carmen opened her eyes wide. She shot an accusing look at Tibby, who just shrugged.

"Yes," Carmen answered stiffly.

"When?"

"August nineteenth. Thanks for caring."

Bailey nodded. "Are you going?"

Carmen pressed her lips together. "No."

"Why not?"

"Because I don't feel like it," Carmen answered.

"Are you mad at your dad?" Bailey asked.

"No, I'm not."

"Then why aren't you going?"

"Because I don't like his new family. They're annoying." Carmen knew she sounded pouty and spoiled.

"Why don't you like them?"

Carmen fidgeted. She switched her legs. "I don't fit in."

"Why not?"

"Because I'm Puerto Rican. I have a big butt." Carmen smiled in spite of herself.

"So are you saying you don't like them or they don't like you?"

Carmen cocked her head. She paused. "I guess both."

"But what about your dad?"

"What do you mean?" Carmen asked.

"I mean, isn't he the one who matters?" Bailey asked.

Carmen stood and waved her hands at Tibby. "Hang on. Hang on. What kind of movie is this?" she demanded.

"It's a documentary," Tibby said.

"Right, but about what?" Carmen asked.

"It's just about people. Stuff that's important to them," Bailey supplied.

"Well, do you really think anybody is going to care about me and my dad?"

Bailey shrugged. "If you do," she said.

Carmen studied her fingernails. They were bitten short, with little hangnails decorating the sides.

"So why did you throw the rocks?" Bailey continued. "You must have been pretty mad."

Carmen's mouth fell open. She glared at Tibby. "Thanks a lot. Do you tell her everything?"

"Only important stuff," Tibby replied.

For some reason, Carmen felt tears welling in her eyes. She didn't blink for fear of pushing them out for the camera to see. "I'm not mad at my dad," she said forcefully.

"Why not?"

249

The tears were bulging now. Sometimes just having tears made you start feeling sorry for yourself and needing to make more. "I'm just not," Carmen said. "I'm not mad at him."

It was no use. The tears spilled out. They chased each other down her cheeks, over her chin, down her neck. Vaguely she heard a clatter and saw that the boom and microphone were on the floor. Bailey was sitting next to her, cupping her elbow in a gesture that conveyed more sympathy than Carmen could understand. "It's okay," Bailey said softly.

Carmen crumpled. She let her head settle against Bailey's head. She should have told this strange little girl to get lost, but she didn't. She lost track of the camera and the movie and Tibby and even the fact that she had arms and legs and that the world was turning.

Before long, Tibby was sitting on the other side of her, holding her around the waist.

"You're allowed to be mad," Bailey said.

It was seven minutes after four, and Bailey hadn't shown up at Wallman's. Tibby looked at the big clock on the wall behind the cash registers just to make sure. Where was she? She'd never arrived even one minute after Tibby's usual shift ended at four.

Tibby went out the automatic doors, felt the blast of heat, and squinted across the street at the 7-

Eleven. Sometimes Bailey played *Dragon Master* with Brian while she waited for Tibby to be done. Today Brian was playing alone. He looked up, and she waved at him. He waved back.

By eighteen after four, Tibby was starting to feel really bothered. She counted on Bailey to hang around her practically every moment of the day. She took it for granted. Sure, she'd minded it at first, but now was different.

Had Bailey gotten stuck at her house, waiting for Loretta to let her in so she could pick up the movie equipment? Had she gotten tired of their movie all of a sudden?

Knowing Bailey, she didn't quite believe any of those things, but they passed the time. She paced for another eight minutes and jumped on her bike. She checked her own house first. No Bailey. She rode back past Wallman's just in case. Then she biked to Bailey's house.

No one answered when Tibby knocked on the door. She rang the bell a few times. She was standing in the middle of the front walk, looking up at Bailey's window for signs of life, when a neighbor passed slowly on the sidewalk.

"Are you looking for the Graffmans?" the woman asked, pausing at the Graffmans' front gate.

"Yeah. For Bailey," Tibby answered.

"I think they went to the hospital a couple of

hours ago," the woman said. She looked pained.

Tibby tempered the feeling of worry that began to clot in her chest. "Is everything okay?" she asked.

"I really don't know," the woman said. "They're at Sibley."

"Thanks," Tibby called, getting back on her bike. She pointed herself in the direction of the hospital and started pedaling fast.

Bailey probably just had one of her checkups, Tibby thought. They were probably just sucking out a few ounces of her blood to make sure the leukemia wasn't doing stuff it wasn't supposed to. Bailey was obviously fine. Sick kids were in bed. Bailey was all over the place.

If, in fact, this was just a checkup, it would be a little weird for her to show up there, Tibby realized as she walked, sweating, into the freezingly air-conditioned lobby.

She paced the lobby, considering her options, then spotted Mrs. Graffman entering the wide hospital doors. She was wearing a suit, and she carried a bag from McDonald's.

"Mrs. Graffman, hi," Tibby said, popping up in Mrs. Graffman's face. "I'm Bailey's friend." Vaguely she remembered her weeks of resistance to letting Bailey call them friends.

Mrs. Graffman nodded and smiled briefly. "Of course I know who you are."

"Is, uh, everything okay?" Tibby asked. She realized her legs were shaking. God, this place was way over-air-conditioned. They'd make you sick here if you weren't already. "Is she just having a checkup or something?" Tibby was walking right alongside Bailey's mother, though she hadn't really been invited to. Who was the stalker now?

Bailey's mom stopped short, and Tibby just about ran past her. "Do you want to sit down with me for a second?" Mrs. Graffman asked.

"Sure. Okay." Tibby studied the woman's face. Her eyes were red and tired. Her mouth was a little like Bailey's.

Mrs. Graffman led Tibby over to a couple of chairs in a quiet corner. She sat down. There was no chair across from Mrs. Graffman, so Tibby sat right next to her and leaned far forward.

"Tibby, I don't know how much you know about what Bailey's been through. I know she doesn't talk about it."

Tibby nodded numbly. "She doesn't talk about it."

"You know she has leukemia. Cancer of the blood."

Tibby nodded again. That seemed like such a bleak way of putting it. "It's pretty treatable, though, right? Don't kids get better from that?"

Mrs. Graffman's head seemed to loll a bit to

the side, like it was getting too heavy to hold up. "Bailey was diagnosed when she was seven. She's had eight rounds of chemotherapy, radiation, and a bone marrow transplant last year. Bailey has spent most of her life in a treatment center in Houston, Texas." She let out a ragged little gasp and then collected herself. "Whatever we do, it keeps coming back."

Tibby was so cold her teeth were chattering. All the little hairs on her arms stood up straight. "Aren't there more treatments they can try? Aren't there?" Tibby's voice came out louder and ruder than she'd intended.

Bailey's mom shrugged with pointy shoulders. "We wanted to give her a couple of months to live in the world like an ordinary kid."

"Are you saying you're just letting her die?" Tibby demanded.

Mrs. Graffman blinked a few times. "We don't know . . . what else to try," she said, her voice squeaky. "Bailey has a bad infection now. We pray her body is strong enough to fight it." She looked up through swollen, teary eyes. "We're very afraid. You need to know that."

Suddenly Tibby's chest hurt. Her breathing felt wrong. Her heart seemed to be leaping around without any particular rhythm.

"Bailey adores you," Mrs. Graffman went on.

The lines at the sides of her mouth quivered. "You've made these two months the most special time of her life. Her father and I really appreciate everything you've done."

"I have to go," Tibby whispered. Her heart was going to explode, and she was going to die herself, and she didn't want to do it in the hospital.

You can take a road
that gets you to the
stars.
I can take a road
that will see me
through.
—Nick Drake

On a morning in early August, Lena shared her customary silent breakfast with Bapi, then packed up and scaled the cliff to the flatland. She was going back to her olive grove. No. His olive grove.

When she reached her spot, she saw that the colors had changed since June. There was more yellow in the grass, different wildflowers. The olives on the trees were grown fatter—they were teenagers now. The breeze was stronger. The *meltimi*, her grandmother called it.

She might have come hoping to see him here; she wasn't sure. But painting stole her thoughts from any other thing. For hours, in deep concentration, she mixed and painted and squinted and painted. If the sun was hot, she stopped knowing it. If her limbs were tired, she stopped feeling them.

When the shadows grew too long, she came

back to regular life. Now she looked at her painting through critical, earthbound eyes. If she hadn't been herself she would have smiled, but as it was, she just felt the smile.

Now she knew what the work had been for. She would give this, her best painting, to Kostos.

She despaired of ever having the courage to tell him how she felt. She hoped this painting would say to him in Lena-language that she recognized that it was his special place, and that she was sorry.

Tibby called in sick to Wallman's. She had a cramp in her foot. She had a twitch in her eye. Her nose ring was getting infected. She just wanted to go to sleep.

She didn't want to be at work and have Bailey be in the hospital. She didn't want to forget even for a moment and have to remember again when Bailey didn't come at four. The forgetting and having to remember again was the very worst part.

She looked longingly into Mimi's glass box. Mimi was sleepier than ever. She hadn't even touched her food. Mimi lived so slowly, and yet her life cycle was progressing much faster than Tibby's. Why was that? Tibby expected her to keep pace.

Tibby went over and tapped the glass wall. She felt an unexpected surge of frustration that Mimi could just snooze through all this distress. She reached into her box and nudged Mimi's soft stomach with her index finger.

Something was wrong. Mimi wasn't right. She wasn't warm. She was room temperature. With a jolt of panic, Tibby grabbed her too roughly. Mimi flopped between Tibby's hands. She didn't stir. "Mimi, come on," Tibby urged her tearfully, like Mimi was playing a stupid guinea pig joke. "Wake up."

Tibby held her up high, in one hand. Mimi hated that. She usually scrambled her sharp little nails against Tibby's wrist.

Dawning on her both slowly and panic-fast was the knowledge that this wasn't Mimi anymore. This was leftover Mimi.

Somewhere in her brain a wall formed, a wall that kept out further consideration about what was happening here. Tibby's thoughts were confined to the small area of her brain that was left. They felt more like commands from a control tower than actual thoughts.

Put Mimi back in her cage. No, don't. She might start to smell. Take her to the backyard.

No way. Tibby bristled at the control tower. She was not doing that.

Should she call her mom at work? Should she call the vet? No, she knew what they would say.

She had a different idea. She marched downstairs. For once in her life her house was quiet.

Without thinking any more than was strictly necessary, she put Mimi in a brown lunch bag, crumpled down the top so she was snug, and stuck her in the freezer.

Suddenly Tibby flashed on the horrible image of Loretta defrosting Mimi and dumping her into a roasting pan. Tibby threw open the freezer door again and hid Mimi behind the frozen remains of Katherine's baptismal cake, which no one would ever eat or throw away.

There. Fine. Mimi wasn't . . . whatever. She was just on ice. There was technology for this kind of thing. There was a whole science, Tibby was pretty sure. It might take a decade to perfect the science, but Tibby wasn't going to be impatient about it. There was time.

Upstairs she collapsed on her bed. She took a pen and notepad from her nightstand to write a letter to Carmen or Bee or Lena, but then she realized she had nothing to say.

Carmen,
      Every day I've been in Greece I've eaten breakfast with my grandfather, and we've never had a single conversation. Is that weird? Does he think I'm a freak? Tomorrow, I swear, I'm going to memorize at least three sentences in Greek and say them. I'll feel

like a failure if the summer ends and we still haven't said a word to each other.

When we get back, do you think you could give me a few pointers on how to be a normal person? I don't seem to get it.

Love,
Lena

Raw and open, Carmen collapsed on her mother's bed and let her mother rub her back.

"My baby," Christina murmured.

"I am mad at Dad," Carmen announced, half into the quilt.

"Of course you are."

Carmen flipped over onto her back. "Why is that so hard for me to say? I have no trouble being mad at you."

"I've noticed that."

Carmen's mom was silent for a while, but Carmen could tell she had something to say.

"Do you think it's easier to be mad at people you trust?" her mom asked very softly.

I trust Dad, Carmen was about to say without thinking. Then she tried thinking. "Why is that?"

"Because you trust that they'll love you anyway."

"Dad loves me," she said quickly.

"He does," her mother agreed. She waited

some more, but with a look of purpose in her eyes. She lay down beside Carmen on her bed. She took a long breath before she started in again.

"It was very hard on you when he moved away."

"It was, wasn't it?" Carmen remembered her seven-year-old self, aping the words her father told her when anyone asked. "He has to go for his job. But we're going to see each other as much as ever. It's the best thing for all of us." Did she really believe those words? Why did she say them?

"You once woke up in the middle of the night and asked me if Daddy knew you were sad."

Carmen rolled onto her side and propped her cheek on her palm. "Do you think he knew?"

Christina paused. "I think he told himself you were okay." She was quiet again. "Sometimes you tell yourself the things you need to hear."

"Tibby, dinner!" It was her dad's voice. He was home.

It was freezing. Tibby shivered in her flannel shirt and pajama bottoms. Her dad must have turned the a/c up again. Ever since her parents had central air-conditioning installed in the house, they had kept the place hermetically sealed four to five months of the year.

"Tibby?"

Dully she realized that she would have to answer him eventually.

"Tibby!"

She opened her door a crack. "I ate already," she yelled through it.

"Why don't you join us anyway," he called. He phrased it like a suggestion, so she figured she could ignore it. She closed her door. She knew that in a few seconds, Nicky would start flinging peas and Katherine would emit one of her arcing vomits—she had baby reflux—and her parents would forget about Tibby, the sullen teenager.

She touched her hair. It wasn't just greasy at the scalp. It was greasy all the way to the ends. She would be leaving a slick on the pillowcase.

"Tibby, honey?" It was her dad still. He wasn't giving up so easily.

"I'll come down for dessert!" she bellowed. Her chances were good he would forget by then.

It was seven. She could watch game shows until the WB shows started. Then those could take her right through ten o'clock. Unlike those emergency room shows, she knew, the WB shows would have no relationship to your actual life. Then there were hours of pompous rockumentaries on VH1 of bands that had died of drug overdoses before she was born. Those were good for putting her to sleep.

The phone rang. The first time Tibby's mom got

263

pregnant, Tibby got her own phone line. The second time, Tibby got her own TV. When the phone rang in here, she knew it was for her. She crawled deeper under her covers.

The times you were in the kitchen and wanted Carmen to call you back, the answering machine picked up after three seconds. When you were screening calls less than two feet from the phone, it rang for hours unanswered. At last the machine clicked on.

"Hi, Tibby? This is Bailey."

Tibby froze. She shrank from the phone.

"My number here is 555-4648. Call me, okay?"

Tibby shivered under the covers. She focused on the commercial about erectile dysfunction. She wanted to go to sleep.

She thought of Mimi downstairs freezing in her little box and her up here freezing in her big one.

Bridget took a long time getting dressed for the big game. Other girls had decorated their shirts with pictures of taco fixings. It was the kind of thing Bridget would have loved if she hadn't run out of steam.

Both teams had strung paper streamers along their goals. There was a table piled with watermelons at the side of the field.

Her cleats felt too loose. Bridget knew she'd lost

some weight. Her metabolism required constant feeding. But could you lose weight in your feet?

"Bridget, where've you been?" Molly asked. Bridget knew there'd been some kind of unofficial kick-around this morning.

"Resting up for the big game," Bridget said.

Molly wasn't sensitive enough to detect anything else, and Bridget didn't want her to.

"All right, Tacos," Molly said. "We've got a tough game here. Los Cocos are on a roll. As you all saw yesterday, they are clicking. We are going to have to max it out to win this."

Bridget made a mental note never to say "max it out."

Molly turned to her, her face full of giving. "You ready, Bee? You do your thing. You go all out today."

The rest of the team cheered at that. Bridget just stood there. She'd been stuck on defense. Stuck in the goal. Screamed at when she dribbled the ball more than two yards. "I don't know if I remember how," she said.

From the first moment, Bridget was slow. She was tentative. She didn't go after the ball. When it came to her she kicked it away. It made her team confused and listless. They were used to building on her intensity. Los Cocos scored twice in the first five minutes.

Molly signaled to the ref for time. She looked at Bridget like she was a stranger. "Come on, Bridget. Play! What's the matter with you?"

Bridget really hated Molly right then. She'd never been great with authority. "You wasted me when I was good. Right now I'm not. Sorry."

Molly was furious. "Are you punishing me?"

"Were you punishing me?"

"I'm the coach, goddammit! I'm trying to turn you from a showoff into a real player."

"I am a real player," Bridget said, and she walked off the field.

What you do speaks
so loudly that I cannot
hear what you say.
—Ralph Waldo Emerson

First Tibby brought up the box of Entenmann's crumb donuts, but then the crumbs reminded her of rodent pellets, so she ran back to the kitchen and shoved them into the back of the cabinet.

Then she thought of ice cream, but she didn't want to go where the ice cream was. Instead she grabbed a box of dinosaur fruit snacks—Nicky's favorite—and brought them upstairs. Her eyes fixed on Ricki Lake, she systematically chewed through eight packages of garish gummy dinosaurs, tossing eight silvery wrappers on the floor.

For *Jerry Springer* she drank two liters of ginger ale. After that she threw up in fizzy Technicolor. After that she watched the shopping network for a while.

Three-quarters of the way through *Oprah*, her phone rang. Tibby turned the volume way up. She hated to miss even one word. Oprah was very sympathetic.

Try as she did to avoid it, Tibby could still hear

the voice on her answering machine. "Uh, Tibby. This is Robin Graffman, Bailey's mom." Long pause. "Do you think you could call or come by? The number is 555-4648. Room 448. Fourth floor, make a left when you get off the elevators. Bailey would really like to see you."

Tibby felt the pain invading her chest again. Her heart was not right. Pain exploded in her temple. She was having a heart attack and a brain aneurysm at the same time.

She looked at Mimi's box. She wanted to curl up in those soft wood shavings and breathe in Mimi's salty rodent smell and sleep until she died. It didn't look hard.

Carmen dialed the numbers. She half expected to hang up when she heard a woman's voice pick up, but she didn't. "Lydia, this is Carmen. May I speak to my father?"

"Of course," Lydia said hastily. Did Carmen seriously think that Lydia would bring up anything unpleasant?

Her father's voice came quickly. "Hello?" She heard both relief and fear in his voice.

"Dad, it's Carmen."

"I know. I'm glad you called." He sounded mostly like he really was glad. "I got the package. I appreciate your thought."

"Oh . . . good," Carmen said. She felt herself being tugged into the comfort zone. She could apologize. He would be overly understanding. In under two minutes, all would be shiny again. Life would go on.

She had to fight on. "Dad, I need to tell you something."

She felt his silent pressure not to do it. Or was it her own pressure? "Okay."

Go go go, she commanded herself. *Don't look back.* "I'm mad at you," she said a little brokenly. She was glad he stayed quiet.

She took a breath and dug into the skin around her thumbnail. "I'm . . . disappointed, you know. I thought we'd be spending the summer together, me and you. I really, really wish you'd warned me about moving in with Lydia's family." Her voice was shaky and raw.

"Carmen, I'm . . . sorry. I wish I'd warned you. That was my mistake. I really am sorry."

He finished with a note of finality. He was closing it off again. Cauterizing the wound before there could be any more bleeding.

She wasn't cooperating. "I'm not finished," she declared. He was silent.

She gave herself a few moments to steady her voice. "You've found yourself a new family, and I don't really fit into it." Her voice came out squeaky and bare. "You got yourself this new family with these new kids. . . . B-But what about me?" Now she was completely off the road and driving fast. Emotions she hadn't even realized she felt were flying past. "What was the matter with me and Mom?" Her voice cracked painfully. Tears were falling now. She didn't even care if he was listening anymore; she had to keep talking.

"Why wasn't your old family good enough? Why did you move away? Why did you promise me . . . we'd be closer than ever?" She broke off so she could try to catch her breath. "W-Why did you keep saying we were, even though it wasn't true?" She was flat-out sobbing now. Her words rose and fell on waves of crying. She wondered if he could even understand what she was saying.

"Why does Paul visit his drunk father every month, and you visit me two or three times a year? I didn't do anything wrong, did I?"

She stopped using words at all and just cried, maybe for a long time; she wasn't sure. At last she got quieter. Was he even there?

When she pressed the receiver to her ear and listened, she heard a muffled sound. Breaths. Not dry, wet.

"Carmen, I'm sorry," he said. "I'm so sorry."

She figured she might believe him, because she realized that for the first time in her life he was crying too.

Tibby was sinking into sleep the next afternoon when

a knock came at the door. "Go away!" she barked.

Who could it be? Her parents were both at work, and Tibby had scared Loretta sufficiently to keep her away forever.

"Tibby?"

"Go away," she said again.

The door opened partway. Carmen's head appeared. As she took in Tibby's horrific appearance and the mounds of crap on the floor and bed, Carmen's face grew pointy with concern. "Tibby, what's going on?" she asked in a soft voice. "Are you okay?"

"I'm fine," Tibby snapped, sinking back under her covers. "Please go away." She turned up the volume. Oprah was coming back after a short commercial break.

"*What* are you watching?" Carmen asked.

With the shades pulled down, there wasn't much to look at besides the TV and the hulking piles of mess.

"Oprah. She's very sympathetic, you know," Tibby snapped.

Carmen waded through the piles and sat on Tibby's bed. It was testament to her concern, because Carmen hated any mess she herself hadn't made. "Tibby, please tell me what's going on. You're scaring me."

"I don't want to talk," Tibby said stonily. "I want you to go away."

The phone started ringing again. Tibby glared at it as though it were a rattlesnake. "Don't touch it," she ordered.

Beeeep, went the answering machine. Suddenly Tibby dove for it, furiously searching for the volume dial. She dropped the whole thing on the carpet.

Still the voice on the machine came through loud and clear. "Tibby. It's Bailey's mother again. I want you to know what's happening here. Bailey's not doing so well. She has an infection and . . ." Tibby could hear the woman sucking in air. Her lungs sounded like they were full of water. "We—we'd just really like you to come. It would mean a lot to Bailey." She sobbed a little and then hung up.

Tibby couldn't look at Carmen. She didn't want to see anything. She could feel Carmen's eyes digging little tunnels into her brain. She felt Carmen's arm come around her shoulders. Tibby looked away. An infinite number of tears hovered behind her eyelids.

"Please just go." Tibby's voice wobbled.

Carmen, being Carmen, kissed the side of Tibby's head and got up to leave.

"Thanks," Tibby whispered after her.

Unfortunately, Carmen, still being Carmen, arrived back in Tibby's room about an hour later without being invited. This time she didn't even knock. She just appeared.

"Tibby, you have to go see her," Carmen said softly, floating in Tibby's half dream at the side of her bed.

"Go away," Tibby ordered groggily. "I can't move."

Carmen let out a long breath. "You can so. I brought you the Pants." She laid them down over Tibby's feet. It was the only place in the room where they wouldn't be swallowed by ravenous mess. "Put them on and go."

"No," Tibby rasped.

Carmen disappeared out the door.

Tibby chattered and shivered. Didn't Carmen understand that her heart wasn't working and her brain had an aneurysm and her nose ring was getting infected?

She fell into comatose sleep for hours and awoke to see the Pants glowing at her in the bluish light of *The Tonight Show with Jay Leno*. The Pants were telling her that she was an awful person, and they were right. She sank back down, feeling the weight of them on her feet and ankles. They seemed to weigh about fifty pounds. Who could walk in such heavy pants? "Surprise yourself," Jay Leno told her. She stared at him. He had not just said that.

She leaped out of bed, scared, her arrhythmic heart racing. What if there was no time left? What if it was already gone?

She pulled off her pajamas and pulled on the Pants. She stuck her feet in a pair of wool clogs. Her hair was so dirty it had gone around the bend. It looked clean again.

She realized once she was out on the sidewalk that it was almost midnight and she was still wearing her pajama top. Who at the hospital would let her in to see Bailey at midnight? Didn't visiting hours end by eight?

She backtracked and got her bike from the open garage. She didn't have very much time. Bailey was afraid of time.

She raced through the streets. The traffic lights on Wisconsin Avenue were flashing yellow.

The regular entrance to the hospital was mostly dark, but the emergency entrance was alight. Tibby walked in and past the assortment of miserable people in plastic chairs. Even emergencies grew boring after people waited for a few hours in this place.

Luckily the woman in the reception box had her head tilted down. Tibby walked right by. She struck out for an elevator.

"Can I help you?" a passing nurse asked her.

"I'm, uh, finding my, uh, mom." Tibby lied badly. She kept walking. The nurse didn't come after her. She took fire stairs up to the main floor, hovered in the stairwell until the coast was completely clear, then sped to the elevator.

There was a tired-looking doctor in the elevator. Tibby rummaged around her brain for excuses, until she realized he really didn't care what she was doing. Obviously he had better things to think about than hospital security.

She got off at the fourth floor and immediately ducked into a doorway. The floor was very quiet. The reception area was to the left, but a sign indicated that room 448 was to the right. There was a nurses' station farther down the hall to the right. She barely breathed as she moved along the wall like a spider. Thank goodness, room 448 was close. The door was partially open. She slipped inside.

She stalled in the little vestibule. From there she could see Jay Leno up on the ceiling-mounted TV doing his shtick in silence. She could see no parents in the chairs by the windows. She had to make herself go in.

She was afraid she would see a different Bailey, a leftover Bailey. But the girl sleeping in the bed was the same as the girl she knew. Only she had tubes sticking out of her wrist and a tube in her nose. Tibby heard a high-pitched little gasp escape her own throat. There was more emotion bubbling around in there than she could hold back.

Bailey was so tiny under the covers. Tibby saw the flutter of pulse at her neck. Gently Tibby reached for Bailey's hand. It was made of bird bones. "Hi, Bailey, it's me," she whispered. "The girl from Wallman's."

Bailey was so small there was enough extra room for Tibby to sit on the bed next to her. Bailey's eyes stayed shut. Tibby brought Bailey's hand to her chest and held it there. When her own eyelids started to droop, she lay back gingerly, resting her head on the pillow next to Bailey's. She felt the soft tickle of Bailey's hair against her cheek. Tears slipped out of her eyes and went sideways into her ears and onto Bailey's hair. She hoped that was okay.

She would just stay here holding Bailey's hand for all time, so Bailey wouldn't be afraid that there wasn't enough of it.

That night was the celebration of *Koimisis tis Theotokou*, the Assumption of the Virgin. It was the biggest Greek Orthodox holiday after Easter. Both Lena and Effie joined their grandparents in the small, plain, lovely church for the liturgy. Afterward there was a small parade, and then the whole town got busy eating and drinking.

Grandma was on the dessert committee, so she and Effie made dozens of trays of *baklava* with every conceivable kind of nut in the filling for the delicate pastries. Grandma had intensified Effie's training now that the summer was almost at an end.

Lena had one glass of strong, rough-tasting red

wine, and it made her feel tired and sad. She went up to her room and sat by her window in the dark, where she could watch the festivities from a bit of a distance. This was the way she liked to enjoy a party.

Down on the sidewalk and in the little plaza a few yards down from Kostos's house, the celebration became more boisterous after sunset. The men drank loads of *ouzo* and got very expansive once the music began. Even Bapi wore a big, silly smile.

Effie drank a few glasses of wine herself. There was no official drinking age in Greece. In fact, even their grandparents pushed wine on Effie and Lena on special occasions, which probably made Effie much less interested in drinking than she would have been otherwise. Tonight, though, Effie was flushed and exuberant. Lena watched her sister dance to a few songs with Andreas the waiter and then sneak off into an alleyway with him. Lena wasn't worried. Effie was carbonated, but under that she was possibly the most sensible person Lena knew. Effie adored boys, but even at fourteen, she didn't abandon herself for them.

Oia, tonight, had two equally vivid full moons, one in the sky and one in the sea. If Lena hadn't known better, she wouldn't have been able to pick the original.

In the moonlight she saw Kostos's face. He didn't notice Lena's absence or care. She felt sure of it.

I wish you cared, Lena told him telepathically, and then wanted to take it back.

She watched Kostos approach her grandmother. On her tiptoes, Valia hugged him and kissed him so hard, Lena wondered if she might strangle him. Kostos looked joyful. He whispered something in Valia's ear that made her smile. Then they began dancing.

Dinky, small-town fireworks erupted from the plaza. In a way, those were the most awe-inspiring kind, Lena decided with a tiny chill. Unlike the Disney World variety, these homemade ones had a sweet crudeness you could respond to. They showed the effort and the danger, while more polished presentations hid it.

Kostos spun Grandma around. Laughing, she managed to keep her feet under her. He ended the song with a dramatic dip, bending Grandma practically in two. Lena had never seen her grandmother look so happy.

Lena studied the faces of the girls on the sidelines. She could tell that Kostos owned the lust of what few local teenage girls there were in Oia, but instead he chose to dance with all the grandmothers, all the women who had raised him, who had poured into him the love they couldn't spend on their own absent children and grandchildren. It was just a poignant fact of island life that whole generations left to set up real lives in other places.

Lena let the tears dribble past her chin and down her neck. She wasn't exactly sure what she was crying for.

Even after the late hour at which the party ended, Lena couldn't sleep. She sat by her window watching the moon. She waited for breezes to feather the edges of the sea-moon. She imagined all the happy inhabitants of Oia falling into deep, drunken sleep.

But as she craned a little out the window, she recognized another pair of elbows in the far window of the second floor. They were Bapi's wrinkly elbows. He was sitting at his window, staring at the moons, just like she was.

She smiled, both inside and out. She'd learned one thing in Santorini. She wasn't like either of her parents or her sister, but she was just like her Bapi— proud, silent, fearful. Lucky for Bapi, he had found the courage once in his life to seize a chance at love from a person who knew how to give it.

Lena prayed on these two moons that she would find that same courage.

All Moanday, Tearday,
Wailsday, Thumpsday,
Frightday, Shatterday.
—James Joyce

Lena slept in the next morning. Well, she didn't sleep in. She stayed in bed hours after she woke, because she couldn't figure out what to do with herself. She was fitful, both energized and apathetic.

Effie ended the morning when she banged in, needing to raid Lena's closet for something or other. "What's the matter with you?" Effie asked over her shoulder while rummaging shamelessly through Lena's things.

"I'm tired," Lena claimed.

Effie looked suspicious.

"How was last night?" Lena asked to deflect attention.

Effie's eyes brightened. "It was unbelievably great," she gushed. "Andreas is the best kisser. Much better than any American boy."

"You mentioned that," Lena pointed out sourly. "Besides, you're fourteen."

Suddenly Effie stopped jangling hangers. She was completely motionless.

"What?" Lena demanded. Effie made her nervous whenever she was quiet.

"Oh my God," Effie breathed.

"What!" Lena shouted.

She cringed when she heard the rustle of paper and saw what Effie was holding. It was the drawing she'd made of Kostos.

"Oh my God," Effie repeated, slower this time. She turned to Lena, as though seeing her sister through new eyes. "I can't believe you."

"What?" Lena's vocabulary seemed to have come down to that one word.

"I *cannot* believe you."

"What?" Lena shouted again, sitting up in bed.

"You are in love with Kostos," Effie accused.

"No I'm not." If Lena hadn't known she was in love with Kostos before, she did now. Because she knew what a lie felt like.

"You are too. And the sad thing is, you are too much of a chicken to do anything about it but mope."

Lena sank into her covers again. As usual, Effie had summed up her complex, anguished mental state in one sentence.

"Just admit it," Effie pressed.

Lena wouldn't. She crossed her arms stubbornly over her pajama top.

"Okay, don't," Effie said. "I know it's true anyway."

"Well, you're wrong," Lena snapped babyishly.

Effie sat down on the bed. Her face was serious now. "Lena, listen to me, okay? We don't have much more time here. You are in love. I've never seen anything like this before. You have to be brave, okay? You have to go and tell Kostos how you feel. I swear to God if you don't, you will regret it for the rest of your cowardly life."

Lena knew this was all true. Effie had hit the mark so blatantly, Lena didn't even bother refuting it. "But, Ef," she said, her voice belying her raw agony, "what if he doesn't like me back?"

Effie considered this. Lena waited, expecting, hoping for reassurance. She wanted Effie to say that *of course* Kostos liked her back. How could he not? But Effie didn't say that.

Instead she took Lena's hand in hers. "That's what I mean about being brave."

Bailey was looking at Tibby when she woke up in the hospital bed. So was the nurse carrying Bailey's breakfast tray. Bailey looked pleased. The nurse looked slightly annoyed.

"I hope you enjoyed your rest," the nurse said, looking up at Tibby from under her eyebrows and giving her a small half-smile.

Tibby slid off the bed. "Sorry," she said groggily. She'd left a spot of drool on Bailey's pillow.

The nurse shook her head. Her face wasn't mean. "Mrs. Graffman was quite surprised to find you here last night," she said to Tibby. "Next time I suggest you try coming during regular visiting hours." She looked from Tibby to Bailey. "I hear you know this young lady."

Bailey nodded. She was still lying back, but her eyes were alert.

"Thanks," Tibby said.

The nurse checked the chart at the bottom of Bailey's bed. "I'll be back in a few minutes in case you need any help with that." She gestured with her eyes toward the breakfast tray.

"I don't," Bailey said.

The nurse gave Tibby a stern glance before she left the room. "Don't eat her breakfast."

"I won't," Tibby promised.

"Come back," Bailey said, bouncing her hand slightly on the bed.

Tibby got back on. "Hi," she said. She almost said, "How are you feeling?" but she managed not to.

"You're wearing the Pants," Bailey observed.

"I needed help," Tibby explained.

Bailey nodded.

"Mimi died." Tibby could not believe she'd said those words. Without warning she started to cry big, sloppy tears.

One delicate tear trailed down Bailey's face. "I knew something was wrong," she said.

"I'm sorry," Tibby said.

Bailey shook her head to fend off the apology. "I knew you were here last night. It gave me good dreams."

"I'm glad."

Bailey looked at the clock. "You have to go. Your shift is starting in thirteen minutes."

"What?" Tibby was genuinely confused.

"Wallman's."

Tibby brushed it aside with her hand. "It doesn't matter."

Bailey looked serious. "It does too matter. It's your job. Duncan counts on you, you know. Go."

Tibby looked at her in disbelief. "You really want me to go?"

"Yes." She softened a little. "I want you to come back, though."

"I will," Tibby said.

When she got to the lobby, Carmen was sitting there. She got up when she saw Tibby and hugged her. Tibby hugged back.

"I have to go to work," Tibby said numbly.

Carmen nodded. "I'll walk you."

"I have my bike."

"So I'll walk you and your bike," Carmen said.

"Oh, wait." Carmen stopped just inside the automatic doors. "I need the Pants."

"Right now?"

"I think so," Carmen said.

"I'm kind of wearing them," Tibby pointed out.

Carmen took her arm and pulled her into the bathroom. She took off her baby-blue flares and offered them to Tibby.

It was further proof of the magic of the Pants, how fantastic Carmen looked in them and how laughably dumb Tibby looked in Carmen's baby-blue ones.

Though Carmen had slept in every morning until at least ten o'clock for the past two weeks, on the morning of August 19, she sprang out of bed with the sun. She knew what she was going to do. She pulled on the Pants, loving the snug, perfect fit around her hips. It felt like they loved her. She pushed her feet into leopard-print slides and quickly fastened the pearl buttons of a black collared shirt. She shook out her voluminous hair, still clean from being washed last night. She jabbed silver hoops through her earlobes.

She left a note for her mom on the kitchen table and heard the phone ringing as she sailed toward the door. It was Mr. Brattle, she could see from the caller ID. She let him ring himself out. She wouldn't torture him today.

She took a bus to the airport, where she picked up an expensive round-trip ticket that she'd reserved last night with her father's "emergencies and books" credit card.

She slept peacefully across three seats on the two-hour flight to Charleston, waking only for the snack. Today, she ate the apple.

She used up some time reading magazines in the Charleston International Airport; then she took a cab to the Episcopal church on Meeting Street. This time the live oaks and beard-trailing pecan trees looked nicely familiar.

She arrived a few minutes before the ceremony was to begin. The ushers had finished ushering, and the congregation was assembled among giant bouquets of purple and white blossoms. She tucked herself anonymously into the shadowed back row. She could recognize two of her aunts in the second row. Her stepgrandmother, whom nobody liked, sat next to her aunts. Otherwise Carmen didn't know a single guest on her father's side of the aisle. It was sad how couples only seemed to have couple friends and lost them all once they stopped being a couple.

Suddenly her father appeared at the side door, tall and distinguished in a tuxedo, with Paul in an identical tuxedo standing by. Paul was his best man, she realized. She waited to feel the bile leak through her, but it didn't. Paul looked so serious about his job as best man. Albert and Paul looked right together with their light hair and matching heights. Her father was lucky, she knew.

The bride music started. First to emerge was Krista, looking like a piece of candy in her dress. She looked nice, Carmen decided. Her skin was so pale it looked blue underneath. The music seemed to notch up in volume, a dramatic pause elapsed, and Lydia appeared.

There was something about a wedding. It didn't matter that Lydia was in her forties and wore a silly dress. She was transformed by grace as she walked up the aisle, and Carmen felt just as moved as she was supposed to. Lydia's smile was the perfect bride's smile, shy but sure. Her father's eyes feasted upon his bride's perfection. Once she arrived beside him, the four family members made a crowded half circle beneath the altar.

Carmen felt a momentary pang, seeing the family arranged like that. *They wanted you there too. You were supposed to be there.*

Carmen let herself be hypnotized by the sawing of the cellist, the smell of the candles, and the drone of the minister. She forgot that she was the daughter of the groom and that she was dressed inappropriately. She left her body and traveled high up into the arches, where she could see everything, the big picture.

It wasn't until they were marching back down the aisle that her father found her eyes and pulled her from the ceiling and into her body. The look on his face made her want to stay there.

Diana somehow managed to make her brownies in the camp kitchen. Ollie tried to give her a back rub. Emily offered to lend Bridget her Discman.

They were all worried about her. She heard them whispering when they thought she was asleep.

She went to dinner with them the next night, just because she was sick of them clucking around her and bringing back care packages. There was a pile of rotting food under her bed.

After dinner, Eric came over and asked her to take a walk with him. It surprised her, coming from the man who would not be caught. She said yes.

They walked over the headlands to the main part of the Coyote beach. In silence they walked past the RVs to a secluded place at the end, where palm trees and cacti took over the sand. The sunset was fiery behind their backs.

"I was worried about you. After the game yesterday and everything . . ." His eyes told her he meant it.

She nodded. "I don't always play well."

"But you've got a spectacular talent, Bridget. You must know that. You know that everybody thinks you're a star."

Bridget liked compliments as well as the next person, but she didn't need this one. She knew how she was.

He dug into the sand. He smoothed the walls of the hole he'd made. "I was worried that what happened between us . . . I was worried that you were hurt by it. Maybe more than I understood at the time."

She nodded again.

"You haven't had much experience with guys, have you?" he asked. His voice was gentle. There was nothing demanding. He was trying to help.

She nodded again.

"Oh. I wish I'd known that."

"I didn't tell you. How could you know?"

He widened the hole in the sand. Then he filled it in again. "You know, Bridget, when I first met you, you were so confident and so . . . sexy with me. I thought you were older than you are. I know better now. You haven't done very much. You're a young sixteen."

"I'm fifteen."

He groaned. "Don't tell me that."

"Sorry. Just being honest," she said.

"Couldn't you have been honest before?"

Bridget's mouth quivered. He looked sorry. He came closer to her and put his arm around her shoulders.

He forged ahead. "Here's what I wanted to tell you. We might not get to talk again, so I want you to remember it. Okay?"

"Okay," she mumbled.

He let out a long breath. "It's a tough admission from a guy who's supposed to be a coach here, so listen up." He looked at the sky for help. "You took my life by storm this summer. You've been in my bed with me every night since that day I first saw you." He put his hand on her hair. "The day we swam together. Running together. Dancing together. Watching you play . . . I know I'm a soccer drone, Bee, but watching you play was a huge turn-on."

She smiled a little.

"That's why you scare the shit out of me. Because you're too pretty and you're too sexy and you're too young for me. You know that too, don't you?"

Bridget wasn't sure if she was too young for him, but she knew she was too young for what she had done with him. She nodded.

"And now, after being so close to you, I can't

be around you and not think about what that feels like."

She was going to cry. Big fat tears quivered in her eyes.

He put his palms on either side of her head. "Bee, listen. Someday, when you're twenty, maybe, I'll see you again. You'll be this hot soccer star at some great school, with a million guys more interesting than I am chasing you down. And you know what? I'll see you and I'll pray you want me still." He held two clumps of her hair in his hands like it was precious stuff. "If I could meet you again, at a different time under different circumstances, I could let myself worship you the way you deserve. But I can't now."

She nodded yet again and let the tears fall.

She wanted his profession of feelings to do the trick. She really did. She knew he wanted that too. Whether he spoke the truth or not, he thought he could make her feel better, and he really, really wanted to.

But it wasn't what she needed. Her need was as big as the stars, and he was down there on the beach, so quiet she could hardly hear him.

Is there world
enough for me?
—Jane Frances

Under the tent in the backyard, Carmen's father hugged her for a long time. When he pulled away his eyes were full. She was glad he didn't say anything. She could tell what he meant.

Lydia hugged her too. It was pure duty, but Carmen didn't care. If Lydia loved her father that much, all the better. Krista pecked her cheek and Paul shook her hand. "Welcome back," he said.

If anyone noticed the fact that she was wearing jeans, they didn't say so.

"Bridal party! Time for formal pictures!" called the photographer's elderly assistant, taking no note of the fragile air. "Bridal party! Please gather under the magnolia!" she cried into Krista's ear. It was as though there were hordes of them rather than just four.

Carmen headed for the drinks table, but her father caught her hand. "Come," he said. "You belong with us."

"But I'm . . ." She gestured toward the Pants.

He waved away her concern. "You look fine," he said, and she believed him.

She posed with the four of them. She posed with Krista and Paul. She posed with Lydia and her dad. She posed with her dad. The old assistant made a sour observation about Carmen's jeans, but nobody else said a word. She couldn't help feeling impressed by Lydia letting her fairy-tale wedding pictures be mucked up by a dark-skinned girl in a pair of blue jeans.

The drinks-and-dinner part of the wedding seemed to rush by. Carmen made small talk with her neurotic aunts until the bride and groom took the floor to loud applause. Shortly afterward, Paul arrived at her chair. "Would you like to dance?" he asked her formally, bowing slightly.

Carmen stood, deciding not to worry that she didn't really know how to waltz. She put her arm through his. On the parquet platform he began whirling her in time with the music.

Suddenly she remembered the girlfriend. She began studying the surrounding tables to see where the poison looks would be coming from. Paul seemed to sense her distraction.

"Where's . . . uh . . ." Suddenly Carmen couldn't think of her actual name.

"Skeletor?" Paul supplied.

Carmen felt her cheeks grow hot. Paul laughed. He had an unexpectedly sweet, hiccupy laugh. Had she really never heard it before?

Carmen bit her lip shamefully. "Sorry," she murmured.

"We broke up," he offered. He didn't appear to be the slightest bit sad.

When the song ended he drew away, and she saw her father striding over. Before Paul left the dance floor, he bent close to her ear. "You make your dad happy," he said, surprising her, as he did pretty much every time he opened his mouth.

Her father pulled her into his grasp and waltzed them along the perimeter of the dance floor.

"You know what I'm going to do?" he said.

"What?" she asked.

"From now on, I'm going to be as honest with you as you've been with me," he said.

"Okay," she agreed, and let the twinkly white lights blur into a smeary snowstorm.

At the end of the night, on her way up to bed, she noticed the dining room window. Smooth glass followed a web of fracture lines to a hole. The pane wasn't fixed, but rather covered by clear plastic and a messy arrangement of silver duct tape. For some reason, this made Carmen feel ashamed and happy at the same time.

Lena,

I finally did something right in these pants. I think Tibby did too. So we're sending them to you with some good Carma attached (heh heh heh). I can't wait to tell you about everything when we're all together again. I hope these pants bring you as much happiness as they brought me today.

Love,
Carmen

Tibby went to work in her pajama top. She had to borrow a smock. Duncan pretended to be surly, but she could tell he was happy to see her after she'd called in sick for so many days. He complimented her on Carmen's pants.

At four o'clock her treacherous mind slipped back into the assumption that Bailey would show up. And then Tibby had to remember again.

"Where's your friend?" Duncan asked. Everybody at Wallman's knew Bailey now.

Tibby went to the back entrance to cry. She sat on the high concrete step and buried her face. Every so often she wiped her flowing nose on the borrowed smock. Her skin was sticky under her flannel pajama top.

Somebody was there. She looked up. It took her a moment to adjust her eyes to the sight of Tucker Rowe.

"Are you okay?" he asked her. Absently she wondered if he ever got hot in all that black.

"Not particularly," she answered. She blew her nose into the smock.

He sat down next to her. She was too deeply into crying to stop, so she just cried like that for a while. Awkwardly he patted her hair once. If she had been her regular self she might have been ecstatic that he was touching her, though mortified that he was touching her filthy hair. As it was, she only gave it a glancing thought.

When the tears finally subsided, she looked up.

"Why don't we get a cup of joe and you tell me what's up," he offered.

She looked at him carefully, not through her eyes but through Bailey's eyes. His hair was overgelled, and his eyebrows were plucked in the middle. His clothes and his reputation seemed fake. She couldn't for the life of her remember why she had liked him.

"No thanks," she answered.

"Come on, Tibby. I'm serious." He thought she was turning him down out of insecurity. As though someone so much cooler than her couldn't possibly take an interest.

"I just don't want to," she clarified.

His face registered the insult.

I used to have a huge crush on you, she thought as she watched him walk away. *But now I can't remember why.*

Not long after he left, Angela, the lady with the long fingernails, came out carrying two clear bags of garbage to the Dumpster. When she saw Tibby she stopped.

"Your little friend is real sick, isn't she?" Angela asked.

Tibby looked up in surprise. "How did you know that?" she asked.

"I had a little niece die of cancer," Angela explained. "I remember how it looks."

Angela's eyes were teary too. She sat down next to Tibby. "Poor thing," she said, patting Tibby's back. Tibby felt the scratchy tips of her fingernails on the polyester.

"She's a sweet, sweet kid, your friend," Angela went on. "One afternoon she was waiting for you. I got off first, and she saw I was upset about something. She took me out for ice tea and listened to me cry for half an hour about my rotten ex-husband. We made it a little Wednesday afternoon ritual, Bailey and I did."

Tibby nodded, feeling equal parts awe for Bailey and disappointment in herself. All she'd ever noticed about Angela were her fingernails.

In a miracle fitting the magic of the Traveling Pants, they arrived in Greece on Lena's last day. The package was so crumpled, it looked as though it had gone around the world and back, but the Pants were there, unharmed—though they were wrinkled and softer and a little more worn than when she'd seen them last. They looked almost as exhausted as Lena felt, but they also looked like they'd hold up for about a million more years. These Pants were Lena's final mandate: Go tell Kostos, you big loser.

As she put them on, they gave her more than guilt. They gave her courage. The Pants mysteriously held the attributes of her three best friends, and luckily bravery was one of them. She would give the Pants what meager gifts she had, but courage was the thing she would take.

She also felt sexy in the Pants, which couldn't hurt.

Lena had once participated in a charity walkathon that took her eighteen miles through Washington, D.C., and its suburbs. Amazingly, the walk to the forge was longer.

She meant to go after lunch, but then she realized she couldn't eat any lunch anyway, so why wait?

Which turned out to be a good thing. When she saw the low building around the bend, she would have thrown up, but she didn't have any food in her stomach, so she managed not to.

Lena's hands were sweating so profusely she was afraid they might smear her painting. She tried drying them on the Pants and switching hands, but wet handprints on your pants weren't exactly the hallmark of a cool customer.

At the entrance to the yard she stopped. *Keep walking*, she silently ordered the Pants. She trusted them more than her actual legs.

What if Kostos was busy working? She couldn't very well bother him, could she? *Whose terrible idea was it to pounce on him at work?* the cowardly part of her brain (representing a very large majority) wanted to know.

She kept walking. The very small, brave part of her brain knew that this would be her one chance. If she turned around, she would lose it.

The forge was dark but for the roaring flames contained in the massive brick firebox at the back. There was one figure working a piece of metal in the fire, and it was too tall to be Bapi Dounas.

Kostos either heard or felt her footsteps. He saw her over his shoulder, then carefully, slowly put down his work, took off his big gloves and mask, and came over to her. His eyes still seemed to carry the slightest reflection of the fire. There was nothing self-conscious or worried in his face. That appeared to be her department.

Lena usually counted on boys being nervous around her so she could claim the natural upper hand, but Kostos wasn't like that.

"Hi," she said shakily.

"Hi," he said sturdily.

She fidgeted, trying to remember her opening line.

"Would you like to sit down?" he offered. Sitting meant perching on a low brick wall that partitioned one part of the room from the other. She perched. She still couldn't remember how to start. She recalled her hand and then the painting in her hand. She thrust it at him. She'd planned a more elaborate presentation, but whatever.

He turned the painting over and studied it. He didn't respond right away like most people; he just looked. After a while that made her nervous. But she was already so nervous it was hard to tell exactly where the extra nervous started.

"It's your place," she explained abruptly.

He didn't take his eyes off the painting. "I've been swimming there many years," he said slowly. "But I'm willing to share it."

She listened for something suggestive in his words—half hoping there was, half hoping there wasn't. There wasn't, she decided.

He handed the painting back to her.

"No, it's for you," she said. Suddenly she felt mortified. "I mean, if you want it. You don't have to take it. I'll just . . ."

He took it back. "I want it," he said. "Thank you."

Lena swept her hair off the back of her neck. God, it was hot in this place. *Okay*, she coached herself, *time to get talking*.

"Kostos, I came here to tell you something," she said. As soon as her mouth opened, she was on her feet, shuffling and pacing.

"Okay," he said, still sitting.

"I've been meaning to since . . . since . . . that day when . . ." *How to put this?* she wondered frantically. ". . . We, uh, ran into each other at the pond."

He nodded. Was there the tiniest suggestion of a smile at the corner of his mouth?

"So. Well. That day. Well." She started pacing again. Her father's lawyerly quickness on his feet was just another of the things she hadn't inherited from him. "There was some confusion and maybe, you know, mistaken ideas about what happened. And that was probably my fault. But I didn't realize it was happening until it had already happened and then . . ." She trailed off. She glanced at the blaze. The flames of damnation weren't the most comforting sight.

Kostos sat patiently.

When Lena started rambling like this, she counted on people to interrupt her and put her out of her misery, but Kostos didn't do that. He just waited.

She tried to get back on track, but she forgot what the track was. "After it happened, it was too late, and everything was even more confused, and I wanted to talk about it, but I couldn't really find the way to talk about it, because I was too much of a coward to make them talk about the thing they thought had happened, and explain that what they thought had happened hadn't really happened, so I didn't do it even though I meant to and I know I should have." She suddenly wished she were in a soap opera, and that somebody would slap her across the face the way they did to people who blathered and raved on daytime TV.

She was now fairly sure she saw the hint of a smile on Kostos's face. That wasn't a good sign, was it?

With the back of her hand she wiped the sweat from her upper lip. She looked down at the Pants, and remembering that they were the Pants, she tried to imagine she was Bridget.

"What I'm really trying to say is that I . . . that I made a huge mistake and that whole crazy fight between our grandfathers was all my fault and I should never have accused you of spying on me, because I know now that you weren't." There, that was better. Oh. But she'd forgotten something. "And I'm sorry," she burst out. "I'm very, very sorry."

He gave her another moment to make sure she was finished. "I accept your apology," he said with a little bow of his head. His manners did the grandmothers in Oia proud.

Lena let out a long breath. Thank the Lord the apology part was done. She could just pack it up and get back home with some small sliver of her pride intact. It was awfully tempting. God, it was tempting.

"There's something else," she told him. She was both appalled and impressed that the words actually came out of her mouth.

"What is it?" he asked. Was his voice more tender now? Did she just wish it were?

She tried to think of good words to say. She looked to the ceiling for assistance.

"Would you like to sit?" he invited again.

"I don't think I can," she answered honestly, wringing her hands.

The expression in his eyes told her he accepted that.

"Well, I know I was not very friendly when I first got here." Lena started in on round two. "You were nice to me, and I was not nice back. And that probably maybe made you think that I didn't . . . that I wasn't . . ." Lena paced in a tight circle and then came back to face him.

Big sweat circles spread from under her arms nearly down to her waist. Sweat covered her upper lip and trickled from her hairline. The combination of extreme heat and extreme nervousness caused red patches to sprout all over her skin.

She'd never trusted a boy to like her for something other than how she looked, but if Kostos did her the unimaginable honor of showing that he cared about her today, she would know it wasn't because she looked good.

"You maybe thought that I didn't like you, but the thing is . . ."

Oh, God. She was going to drown in her own perspiration. Was that possible?

"But the thing is maybe it didn't really mean that at all. Maybe it turned out to mean . . . the completely opposite thing." Was she still speaking English? Were there any sentences coming together?

"So what I'm saying is, I wish I hadn't acted that way to you. I wish I hadn't acted like I didn't like you or didn't care, because I really do . . . I really do . . . not feel like how I maybe seemed like I might feel."

She looked at him with pleading eyes. She had tried, she really had. She was afraid it was the best she could do.

His eyes were as full as hers were. "Oh, Lena," he said. He took both her sweaty hands in his. He seemed to understand that it was the best she could do.

He pulled her close to him. With him perched on the wall and her standing, they were almost the same height. Her legs touched his. She could smell his slightly ashy boy smell. She felt like she might faint.

His face was right there, beautiful and shadowy in the flickering light. His lips were right there. With a courage possessed somewhere not within her body, she leaned forward ever so slightly and kissed his lips. It was a kiss and a question.

He answered the question by pulling her into him, pressing her body tightly against his with both arms, and his kiss was long and deep.

She had one last thought before she left off thinking and gave herself over to feeling. *I never imagined heaven would be so hot.*

In your eyes I am
complete.
—Peter Gabriel

As they had the past two nights, the nurses kicked Tibby out of Bailey's room when visiting hours ended at eight. She wasn't ready to go home yet. She called her mom and told her she was going to a movie. Her mom sounded relieved. Even she'd noticed that Tibby hadn't been having a lot of fun.

Tibby saw the lights of the 7-Eleven in the distance, and they beckoned to her. Inside she was glad to see Brian McBrian hunched over *Dragon Master.*

When he turned around and saw her watching him, he smiled broadly. "Hi, Tibby," he said shyly. He took not even the slightest notice of her pajamas or her horrifying appearance.

"What level?" she asked.

He didn't try to mask his pride. "Twenty-five."

"No way!" she said appreciatively.

She watched with tingly suspense his long

heroic battle through the volcano of level twenty-six, until he got sizzled in lava.

"Awww," she said.

He shrugged happily. "That was a good one. You wouldn't want to win all the time."

She nodded. She thought for a while. "Hey, Brian?"

"Yeah?"

"Will you teach me how to play *Dragon Master*?"

"Sure," he said.

With the patience and enthusiasm of a true teacher, Brian coached her all the way up to level seven, the first dragon. Even as her curvaceous heroine perished with a sword through her belly, he beamed with pride. "You're a natural dragon slayer," he praised her.

"Thank you," she said, feeling truly grateful for the compliment.

"How's Bailey?" he asked her, his face going grave.

"She's in the hospital," Tibby told him.

He nodded. "I know. I've been visiting her at lunchtime." He suddenly had an idea. "Wait a second; I want to show you something." He retrieved a dilapidated backpack. "I got this for her."

Tibby looked. It was a Sega Dreamcast machine and a copy of *Dragon Warrior*, the home version of *Dragon Master*. "It's not as good as the

311

real thing," he explained. "But it will keep her in practice."

Tibby felt tears spring into her eyes. "She'll love it," she said.

Later, as Tibby walked down Old Georgetown Road, she carried a leftover high from her game of *Dragon Master*. She was already thinking about level eight. It was the first time in days she had felt that particular feeling of looking forward to something.

Maybe, she thought as she walked, Brian McBrian was onto something important. Maybe happiness didn't have to be about the big, sweeping circumstances, about having everything in your life in place. Maybe it was about stringing together a bunch of small pleasures. Wearing slippers and watching the Miss Universe contest. Eating a brownie with vanilla ice cream. Getting to level seven in *Dragon Master* and knowing there were twenty levels to go.

Maybe happiness was just a matter of the little upticks—the traffic signal that said "Walk" the second you got there—and downticks—the itchy tag at the back of your collar—that happened to every person in the course of a day. Maybe everybody had the same allotted measure of happiness within each day.

Maybe it didn't matter if you were a world-famous heartthrob or a painful geek. Maybe it didn't matter if your friend was possibly dying.

Maybe you just got through it. Maybe that was all you could ask for.

It was her last breakfast with Bapi, her last morning in Greece. In her frenetic bliss that kept her up till dawn, she'd scripted a whole conversation in Greek for her and Bapi to have as their grand finale of the summer. Now she looked at him contentedly munching on his Rice Krispies, waiting for the right juncture for launch time.

He looked up at her briefly and smiled, and she realized something important. This was how it was supposed to be. This was how they both liked it. Though most people felt bonded and comforted by conversation, Lena and Bapi were two of the kind who didn't. They bonded by the routine of just eating cereal together.

She promptly forgot her script and went back to her cereal.

At one point, when she was down to just milk, Bapi reached over and put his hand on hers. "You're my girl," he said.

And Lena knew she was.

Tibby sat in her usual spot on Bailey's bed two days later, and she knew Bailey was getting worse. Bailey didn't look scared or solemn, but the nurses and nurses' aides did. They dropped their eyes every time Tibby looked directly at one of them.

Bailey was playing *Dragon Warrior* as her dad snoozed in a chair by the window. She tipped her head back on the pillow, clearly needing a rest. "Will you play for me?" she asked Tibby.

Tibby nodded and took over the controls.

"When are your friends getting back?" Bailey asked in a sleepy voice.

"Carmen is home again. Lena and Bridget will be back next week."

"That's nice," Bailey said. Her eyes were closing for longer and longer periods of time.

Tibby noticed there were two more beeping monitors in the room today.

"How's Brian?" Bailey asked.

"He's great. He got me to level ten," Tibby said.

Bailey smiled. She left her eyes closed. "He's a worthwhile guy," she murmured.

Tibby laughed, remembering the phrase. "He is. You were right and I was wrong. Like always."

"Not true," Bailey said. Her face was as white as an angel's.

"It is too true. I judge people without knowing them," Tibby said.

"But you change your mind," Bailey said, her voice slow and drifting.

Tibby paused at the controls of *Dragon Warrior*, thinking Bailey was asleep.

"Keep playing," Bailey ordered in a whisper.

Tibby kept playing until eight o'clock, when the nurses kicked her out.

Lena,
Something happened. It isn't how I imagined. I need to talk to you, but I can't say it here. I'm just . . . strange. I'm strange to myself.

Bee

Lena,
I can't sleep. I'm scared. I wish I could talk to you.

Lena read Bridget's letters on the flight from Athens. Both the ones she'd been getting throughout the summer, and the ones she'd picked up at the post office on the way to the airport. The plane cruised through time zones, and Lena's heart made the painful journey from the forge in Oia, where she wanted it to be, to a girls' soccer camp in Baja, where she felt it was needed.

Lena had known Bee well enough and long enough to be worried. She knew Bee's life had been remade at one time. There were fault lines from then. Bee sprinted along in a torrent of activity, but once in a while something unexpected slammed her hard. It left Bee slow and uncertain. She fretted. She wasn't good at putting herself back together. Bridget was like a toddler sometimes. She grasped for power. She demanded it. But when she got her way, she was left only with herself, and that terrified her. Her mom was gone, and her dad was timid and out of touch. She needed to know someone was looking out for her. She needed someone to promise her that the world wasn't empty.

Effie snored next to her. Lena turned and pushed her sister's shoulder. "Hey, Eff? Eff?"

Effie smiled in her sleep. Lena suspected she was thinking about the waiter. She pushed her shoulder harder. "Effie. Wake up a minute."

Grudgingly, Effie opened her eyes. "I'm sleeping," she complained, like it was a sacrament or something.

"You're good at sleeping, Effie, I'm sure you'll do more."

"Ha-ha."

"Listen, I think I need to change my travel plan, okay? I'm going to leave you in New York, and try to get a flight to Los Angeles."

Effie wasn't a happy flier. Lena knew it was only fair to give her warning. "New York to D.C. is a really short flight, Ef. You'll be fine."

Effie looked stunned. "Why, though?"

"Because I'm worried about Bee." Effie knew Bridget well enough to know that there came low times when worrying about her wasn't frivolous.

"What did she do?" Effie asked, worried herself.

"I don't know yet."

"Do you have money?" Effie asked.

"I still have what Mom and Dad gave us," Lena said. Their parents had given them each $500 for spending money for the summer, and Lena had spent hardly any of it.

"I have two hundred dollars left. You can have it," Effie said.

Lena hugged her. "I'll bring her back home tomorrow. I'll call Mom and Dad from the airport, but will you explain it to them too?"

Effie nodded. "You go be her mother."

"If she needs one," Lena said.

She was glad she'd thought to pack the Traveling Pants in her carry-on bag.

When the phone rang at ten o'clock the next morning, Tibby knew what it was. She picked up the phone and heard sobbing.

"Mrs. Graffman, I know what happened. You don't have to say." Tibby put her hand to her eyes.

The funeral was two days later, on a Monday. There was a graveside service and burial. Tibby stood with Angela and Brian and Duncan and Margaret. Carmen was home from South Carolina. She stood at the back. They all cried quietly.

That night, Tibby couldn't sleep. She watched *Steel Magnolias* on the Movie Channel from one to three A.M.

She was actually happy to hear Katherine yelping at three fifteen. Quietly, before either of her exhausted parents woke up, she went into the nursery and plucked the baby out of her crib and walked her down to the kitchen. She clamped Katherine around her small middle and rested the baby against her shoulder. With the other arm she warmed her bottle. Katherine made singing noises that tickled her ear.

She tucked Katherine into bed with her and watched her fall asleep halfway through her milk. She snuggled around her sister and cried. The tears soaked into Katherine's fuzzy, soft hair.

When Katherine reached the stage of deep baby sleep that could withstand even loud explosions, Tibby put her back into her crib.

Now it was four A.M. Tibby went down to the kitchen. She opened the freezer door and found the brown paper bag that held Mimi. Feeling like she belonged to another world, she walked out to the garage in her pajamas and slippers. She wrapped the top of the bag around the handlebar of her bike, held on tightly, and rode the several miles to the cemetery, frozen Mimi swinging under her wrist.

The ground over Bailey's coffin was still soft. Tibby pushed aside the carpet of grass and dug into the soil with both hands. She kissed the paper bag and planted Mimi in the hole. Then she covered her over and put the grass back in place. She sat down on the grass over the two of them. She saw how pretty the moon looked, falling low on the horizon. A big part of her wanted to just stay here with them. She wanted to curl up into the smallest, simplest possible existence and let the world rush along without her.

She lay down. She curled up. And then she changed her mind.

She was alive, and they were dead. She had to try to make her life big. As big as she could. She promised Bailey she would keep playing.

Lena's sense of time and space was hopelessly scrambled by the time she arrived in Mulege. She had to hire a second cab to take her to the camp. The sun had set, but the air was still hot and thick. She was thousands of miles from Oia, but she breathed the same air.

Lena knew Bridget was scheduled to leave tomorrow, and she needed to be there in time to help get her home—whatever that would entail. She found her way to the administrative office, and from there got directions to Bridget's cabin.

Entering the dimly lit cabin, her eyes immediately found Bridget. Just a yellow head and a dark sleeping bag.

Bridget sat up. Lena took in her tragic face. Her fairy-tale hair. "Hey, Bee," she said, rushing to hug her.

Bridget was having trouble understanding what was going on. She blinked at Lena. She squinted. She hugged her back like she wasn't sure whom she was hugging.

"How did you get here?" Bridget asked in astonishment.

"On a plane."

"I thought you were in Greece."

"I was. Yesterday. I got your letters," she explained.

Bridget nodded. "You really did."

Suddenly Lena took note of the fact that dozens of eyes gazed at them curiously. "Do you want to take a walk?"

Bridget got out of her sleeping bag. She led the way out of the cabin in her oversized T-shirt and her bare feet. Bee never did care much about how she looked.

"This is beautiful," Lena said. "I've watched

the same moon all summer."

"I can't believe you came all the way here," Bridget said. "Why did you come?"

Lena dug her toes into the sand. "I wanted you to know that you weren't alone."

Bridget's eyes were huge and shiny in her face.

"Hey, look what I brought for you," Lena said, pulling the Pants out of her bag.

Bridget clutched them in both arms for a moment before she put them on.

"Tell me what happened, okay?" Lena said, sitting down on the sand, pulling Bridget down next to her. "Tell me everything that happened, and we'll figure out how to fix it."

Bridget looked down at the Pants, grateful to have them. They meant support and they meant love, just as they'd all vowed at the beginning of the summer. But with Lena right here, right next to her, she almost didn't need them.

Bridget looked up at the sky. She looked at Lena. "I think maybe you already did."

We will go · Nowhere
we know · We don't
have to talk at all
—Beck

EPILOGUE

Tradition called for our annual late-night celebration at Gilda's to fall on the middle day between birthdays—nine days after Lena's and nine days before mine, two days after Bridget's and two days before Tibby's. I always find comfort in numbers. I always interpret coincidences as little clues to our destiny. So today it felt like God Himself practically wrote it into my Day Runner. The celebration this year happened to fall the night before school started again, which was significant too, if not in a happy way.

Like salmon swimming back to the tiny tributary where they were spawned, we returned to Gilda's as the honorary birthplace of the Septembers and now of the Sisterhood.

As usual, Tibby and Bee collaborated on the birthday cake, and Lena and I created the mood with decorations and music. Bee always got to do the breaking and entering.

Usually by this time in the summer, we were as worn in to one another as pebbles in a riverbed. For three months we'd had complete togetherness and not much outside stimuli. What few stories we had, we'd considered, analyzed, celebrated, cursed, and joked into sand.

Tonight was different. I felt like we were each separate and full to our edges with our own stories, mostly unshared. In a way it scared me, having a summer of experiences and feelings that belonged to me alone. What happened in front of my friends felt real. What happened to me by myself felt partly dreamed, partly imagined, definitely shifted and warped by my own fears and wants. But who knows? Maybe there is more truth in how you feel than in what actually happens.

The Pants were the only witness to all of our lives. They were the witness and the document too. In the last few days we'd made our inscriptions, telling a little of the story with pictures and words that stood out bright against humble denim.

Tonight I looked around at my friends, sitting on a red blanket, surrounded by candles in the middle of a crummy aerobics studio. Usually the centerpiece was the cake, but tonight it was pushed off to the side in deference to the Pants. Two tan faces and Tibby's pale one looked back at me. Their eyes were all the same color in this light. Tibby gamely wore the sombrero from Mexico and the T-shirt Lena had painted for her showing the harbor at Ammoudi. Lena wore shoes she'd borrowed from Bridget, and Bridget stuck her bare feet toward the center, displaying toenails bright with my favorite turquoise polish. Tibby's and Lena's knees touched. We were settling into one another again, sharing our lives.

But we were quieter tonight. There was more care and less ordinary teasing. In a way, we were still strange to one another, I realized, but there was comfort in the Pants. The Pants had absorbed the summer. Maybe it was better that they couldn't talk. They would let us remember more how we had felt, and less what had actually happened. They would let us keep it all and share it.

It wasn't that we hadn't shared the big outlines of our stories. Of course we had. I told them all about how Al's wedding was. We knew that Bee had messed herself up over Eric. We all saw Lena talk about Kostos in a way she'd never talked about a boy before. We knew about Bailey, and we knew intuitively to be careful when we asked Tibby questions. But there were a million little lines of shading that we couldn't convey so easily. They were the subtle things, and understanding them, even knowing when you missed them, was what separated other friends from real friends, like we were.

Still, the Pants promised us there was time. Nothing would be lost. There was all year if we needed it. We had all the way until next summer, when we would take out the Traveling Pants and, together or apart, begin again.

The Second Summer of the Sisterhood

With a bit of last summer's sand in
their pockets, the Traveling Pants and
the sisterhood that wears them embark
on their sixteenth summer.

Available

everywhere!

Turn the page for an

excerpt from the book....

Nothing is too

wonderful to be

true.

—Michael Faraday

PROLOGUE

Once there were four girls who shared a pair of pants. The girls were all different sizes and shapes, and yet the pants fit each of them.

You may think this is a suburban myth. But I know it's true, because I am one of them — one of the sisters of the Traveling Pants.

We discovered their magic last summer, purely by accident. The four of us were splitting up for the first time in our lives. Carmen had gotten them from a secondhand place without even bothering to try them on. She was going to throw them away, but by chance, Tibby spotted them. First Tibby tried them; then me, Lena; then Bridget; then Carmen.

By the time Carmen pulled them on, we knew something extraordinary was happening. If the same pants fit — and I mean really fit — the four of us, they aren't ordinary. They don't belong completely to the world of things you can see and touch. My sister, Effie, claims I don't believe in magic, and maybe I didn't then. But after the first summer of the Traveling Pants, I do.

The Traveling Pants are not only the most beautiful pair of jeans that ever existed, they are kind, comforting, and wise. And also they make you look really good.

We, the members of the Sisterhood, were friends before the Traveling Pants. We've known each other since before we were born. Our mothers were all in the same pregnancy aerobics class. I feel this explains something about us. We all have in common that we got bounced on our fetal heads too much.

We were all born within seventeen days of each other. You know how people make a big deal about which twin was born three minutes before the other one? Like it matters? Well, we're like that. We draw great significance from the fact that I'm the oldest—the most mature, the most maternal—and Carmen is the baby.

Our mothers started out being close. We had a group play date running at least three days a week until we started kindergarten. Our mothers would gab in whoever's yard it was, drinking iced tea and eating cherry tomatoes. We would play and play and play and occasionally fight. Honestly, I remember my friends' mothers almost as well as my own from that time.

We four, the daughters, reminisce about it sometimes—we look back on that period as a golden age. Gradually, as we grew, our mothers' friendship disintegrated. Then Bee's mother died. A giant hole was left, and none of them knew how to bridge it. Or maybe they just didn't have the courage.

The word *friends* doesn't seem to stretch big enough to describe how we feel about each other. We forget where one of us starts and the other one stops. When Tibby sits next to me in the movies, she bangs her heel against my shin during the funny or scary parts. Usually I don't even notice until the bruise blooms the next day. In history class Carmen absently grabs the loose, pinchy skin at my elbow. Bee rests her chin on my shoulder when I'm trying to show her something on the computer, clacking her teeth together when I turn to explain something. We step on each other's feet a lot. (And, okay, I do have large feet.)

Before the Traveling Pants we didn't know how to be together when we were apart. We didn't realize that we are bigger and stronger and longer than the time we spend together. We learned that the first summer.

And all year long, we waited and wondered what the second summer would bring. We learned to drive. We tried to care about our schoolwork and our PSATs. Effie fell in love (several times), and I tried to fall out of it. Brian became a regular fixture at Tibby's house. Carmen and Paul evolved from stepsiblings to friends. We all kept our nervous, loving eyes on Bee.

While we did our thing, the Pants lived quietly in the top of Carmen's closet. They were summer Pants—that's what we had all agreed on. We had always marked our lives by summers. Besides, with the no-washing rule, we didn't want to overuse them. But not a day of fall, winter, or spring went by when I didn't think about them, curled up in Carmen's closet, safely gathering their magic for when we needed them again.

This summer began differently than the last. Except for Tibby, who'd be going to her film program at a college in Virginia, we thought we'd be staying home. We were all excited to see how the Pants worked when they weren't traveling.

But Bee never met a plan she didn't like to change. So from the start, our summer did not go the way we expected.

oh, who can tell,

save he whose heart

hath tried,

—Lord Byron

Bridget sat on the floor of her room with her heart pounding. On the carpet lay four envelopes, all addressed to Bridget and Perry Vreeland, all with Alabama postmarks. They were from a woman named Greta Randolph, her mother's mother.

The first letter was five years old, and asked them to attend a memorial service in honor of Marlene Randolph Vreeland at the United Methodist church in Burgess, Alabama. The second was four years old, and told Bridget and Perry that their grandfather had died. It included two uncashed checks for one hundred dollars apiece, explaining that the money was a small bequest from their grandfather's will. The third was two years old and included a detailed family tree of the Randolph and Marven families. *Your Heritage* Greta had written across the top. The fourth letter was a year old, and it invited Bridget and Perry to please come visit whenever they could.

Bridget had never seen or read any of them until today.

She'd found them in her father's den, filed with her birth certificate and her report cards and her medical records as though they belonged to her, as though he'd given them to her.

Her hands were shaking when she went into his room. He was just home from work, sitting on the bed and taking off his work shoes and black socks as he always did. When she was very small, she'd liked to do it for him, and he'd liked to say it was his favorite thing in the day. Even at the time it had made her worry that there weren't enough happy things in his days.

"Why didn't you give these to me?" she yelled at him. She strode close enough for him to see what she held. "They are written to me and Perry!"

Her father looked at her like he could barely hear her. He looked that way no matter how loudly she talked. He shook his head. It took him some time to figure out what Bridget was flapping in his face. "I am not on speaking terms with Greta. I asked her not to contact you," he said at last, as if it were simple and obvious and not a big deal.

"But they're mine!" Bridget shouted. It *was* a big deal. It was a very big deal to her.

He was tired. He lived deep inside his body. Messages took a long time to get in and get out. "You're a minor. I'm your parent."

"But what if I had wanted them?" she shot back.

Slowly he considered her angry face.

She didn't feel like waiting around for an answer, letting him set the pace of the conversation. "I'm going there!" she shouted at him without even thinking about what she was saying. "She invited me and I'm going."

He rubbed his eyes. "You're going to Alabama?"

She nodded defiantly.

He finished with his socks and shoes. His feet seemed small. "How are you going to manage that?" he asked her.

"It's summer. I've got some money."

He thought about it. He couldn't seem to think of a reason why she couldn't. "I don't like or trust your grandmother," he told her finally. "But I'm not going to try to forbid you to go."

"Good," she snapped.

She went back to her room as her old summer dissolved and her new one dawned all around her. She was going to go. It felt good to be going someplace.

✼   ✼   ✼

"So guess what?"

This was a phrase from Bee that always made Lena sit up and listen. "What?"

"I'm going away. Tomorrow."

"You're going away tomorrow?" Lena repeated dumbly.

"To Alabama," Bee said.

"You're kidding me." Lena was only saying that. It was Bee, so Lena knew she wasn't kidding.

"I'm going to see my grandmother. She sent me some letters," Bee explained.

"When?" Lena asked.

"Well . . . actually . . . five years ago. That's when the first one came."

Lena was stunned not to have known this.

"I just found them. My dad never gave them to me." Bee didn't sound mad. She stated it as a fact.

"Why not?"

"He blames Greta for all kinds of stuff. He told her not to contact us. He was annoyed that she tried."

Lena had so little optimism where Bee's dad was concerned that this did not shock her.

"For how long, do you think?" she asked.

"I don't know. A month. Maybe two." She paused. "I asked Perry if he wanted to come with me. He read the letters, but he said no."

Lena didn't find that surprising either. Perry had been a sweet kid, but he'd grown into a reclusive teenager.

Lena felt alarmed at this change in plans. They were supposed to get jobs together. They were supposed to hang out all summer. But at the same time she felt oddly comforted by the impulsiveness. It was something the old Bee would do.

"I'll miss you." Lena's voice wobbled a little. She felt weirdly teary. It was natural that she would miss Bee. But Lena usually registered that something was sad before she felt it. Now the order was reversed. It took her by surprise.

"Lenny, I'll miss *you*," Bee said quickly, tenderly, as startled as Lena was by the ready emotion in Lena's voice.

Bee had changed so much in the last year, but a few things had stayed the same. Most people, including Lena herself, backed away when they sensed some out-of-control emotion. Bee went right out to meet it. Right now, that was a thing Lena loved.

Tibby was leaving the next day, and she hadn't finished packing or begun shopping for their biannual break-and-enter at Gilda's. She was madly packing when Bridget appeared.

Bridget sat atop Tibby's bureau and watched

her throw the entire contents of her desk on the floor. She couldn't find her printer cable.

"Try the closet," Bridget suggested.

"It's not there," Tibby answered gruffly. She couldn't open her closet because it was jammed with things she could neither keep nor throw away (like her old guinea pig's cage). Tibby feared that if she even cracked open the door, the whole mountain would tumble and crush her to death.

"I bet Nicky took it," Tibby muttered. Nicky was her three-year-old brother. He took her stuff and broke her stuff, usually the moment before she really needed it.

Bee didn't say anything. She was being awfully quiet. Tibby turned to look at her.

If a person hadn't seen Bee in a year, they might not have recognized her sitting there. She wasn't blond and she wasn't thin and she wasn't moving. She had tried to dye her hair really dark, but the dye she'd used had barely conquered the famous yellow struggling underneath. Bee was normally so thin and muscled that the fifteen or so pounds she'd gained over the winter and spring sat heavily and obviously on her arms and legs and torso. It almost looked like her body wasn't willing to incorporate the extra fat. It just let it sit there, right on the surface, hoping it would go away soon. Tibby couldn't help thinking that what Bee's mind wanted and what her body wanted were two different things.

"I may have lost her," Bee said solemnly.

"Lost who?" Tibby asked, looking up from the mess.

"Myself." Bee bounced one heel against a closed drawer.

Tibby stood. She abandoned her mess. Gingerly she backed toward her bed and sat down, keeping an eye on Bee. This was a rare mood. Month after month Carmen had subtly tried to pry introspection out of Bee, but it hadn't come. Lena had been maternal and sympathetic, but Bee hadn't wanted to talk. Tibby knew this was important.

Although Tibby was the least physical of the group, she wished Bee were sitting next to her. And yet she knew intuitively that Bee was sitting on her bureau for a reason. She didn't want to be sitting on a low, soft place within easy range of comfort. She also knew that Bee had chosen Tibby for this conversation because as much as Tibby loved her, she would listen without overwhelming her.

"How do you mean?"

"I think about the person I used to be, and she seems so far away. She walked fast, I walk slow. She stayed up late and got up early, I sleep. I feel like if she gets any farther away, I won't be connected to her at all anymore."

Tibby's desire to go closer to Bee was so strong she had to clamp her elbows against her legs to make them stay put. Bee's arms were wrapped around her body, containing her.

"Do you want . . . to stay connected to her?" Tibby's words were slow and quiet, seeming to make their way to Bridget one at a time.

Bee had made every effort to change herself this year. Tibby quietly suspected she knew the reason. Bee couldn't outrun her troubles, so she'd entered her own version of the witness protection program. Tibby knew how it was to lose someone you loved. And she also knew how tempting it was to cast off that sad, ruined part of yourself like a sweater you'd outgrown.

"Do I want to?" Bee thought about the words carefully. Some people (like Tibby, for instance) tended to listen in a muffled, sheltered way. Bee was the opposite.

"I think I do." Tears flooded Bee's eyes, gluing her yellow eyelashes into triangles. Tibby felt tears fill her own eyes.

"You need to find her then," Tibby said, and her throat ached.

Bee stretched out one arm and left it out there, her palm turned up to the ceiling. Tibby got up without thinking and took the hand. Bee laid her head on Tibby's shoulder. Tibby felt the softness of Bee's hair and the moisture from her eyes against her collarbone.

"That's why I'm going," Bee said.

Later, when Tibby pulled away from Bee, she wondered about herself. She wasn't as destructive as Bee. She had never been as dramatic. Rather, she'd slipped carefully, stealthily away from her ghosts.